THE YELLOW JOCK CHRONICLES

Volume Two: Jockstrap Branded

A Journey into Self-Awareness, Discovery and Acceptance:
Further Obsession with Jockstraps and Piss-Lust

First Edition

Published by The Nazca Plains Corporation
Las Vegas, Nevada
2007

ISBN: 978-1-934625-30-9

Published by
The Nazca Plains Corporation ®
4640 Paradise Rd, Suite 141
Las Vegas NV 89109-8000

PUBLISHER'S NOTE
The Yellow Jock Chronicles – Volume Two is a work of fiction created wholly by *Matthew M. Schiffmann's* imagination. All characters are fictional and any resemblance to any persons living or deceased is purely by accident. No portion of this book reflects any real person or events.

Cover, Fleshblack Images
Art Director, Blake Stephens

DEDICATION

For "Dean"
Requiescat in Pacem
Et Lux Perpetua Luceat Eis.

THE YELLOW JOCK CHRONICLES

Volume Two: Jockstrap Branded

A Journey into Self-Awareness, Discovery and Acceptance:
Further Obsession with Jockstraps and Piss-Lust

First Edition

Matthew M. Schiffmann

CONTENTS

SUMMER JOB

Summer began with the onset of prairie heat in May. I had secured a post with the Curator in the University Libraries; but the job wouldn't begin until late August. Meanwhile I needed something of a livelihood and took a summer job at the transit terminal out near the airport. Being a shift supervisor basically meant that I could read and write, something not to be taken for granted at Hennepin Transfer and Terminal, so I'd keep the logs of what loads were coming and going from my assigned bays.

Quickly, though, it became clear that I would also be called upon for other duties: helping with loading sometimes, directing the flow of traffic out of the facility, making some fairly important decisions regarding operations. I also realized that the more I agreed to do for the truckers and the administration, the more they would be asking and *expecting* me to do. I decided I would accept spur-of-the-moment tasks only if they were absolutely necessary; otherwise, playing stupid was a better idea.

Of course, seeing truckers and laborers coming in and out all day had its good points too. Usually the guys were pretty sleazy, and if not total trash to start with, they were so groady from days of driving I had no interest anyhow. But there are always exceptions. The terminal had good facilities, so it wasn't uncommon to see a nasty dirt-ball heading into the building only to emerge 90 minutes later as a hot hunk of a road-warrior. I also quickly learned to interpret the subtle signs among truckers and dock hands indicating their 'interests' and willingness for action, boot tapping, keys, stance, and of course the hanky-code.

Some of them were far more obvious. I was all but floored when one big guy came in wearing a brightly printed T-shirt from none other than The Cell Block in Chicago. I stayed away from him. I figured if he was that open about it in the damn truck stop, he probably *liked* to throw down and duke it out as foreplay or something. Maybe pound the shit out of straight truckers and then rape them for fun... such guys *are* out there.

There were the restroom boys. I avoided that scene completely. Even if I had been interested in a particular guy, I couldn't afford a suggestion that I might be cruising the glory-holes or the shower rooms. There were the lot-lizards: mostly women hooking in the parking lot. I hadn't been there three days and the station manager sent a squad of goons out to round up five or six of the cunts and send them running. I learned that this happened about every other week. They'd scatter, then come back later, usually within a day, sometimes within an hour or two.

There were local call-boys. They'd post their phone numbers here and there in the facility, in stalls in the johns, beside the bulletin boards, at the tables in the coffee shop. There was a whole 'nother code for that stuff. I saw a couple of those boys that appeared to be maybe 18; some of the truckers liked 'em like that. When I got a look at them up close though, I realized they were more like 24... and working hard to keep themselves slick and 'young.' One was a Vietnamese refugee; he could pass for a child and had difficulty buying beer even with his ID, but in fact was well into his 30's.

And two of the call-boys were really call-girls. Or maybe the other way around? Anyhow, their level of 'drag' was so refined, so convincing that I heard of a number of instances where burly butch truckers had actually engaged them, used them, paid them and been happy with it, and never even known they'd fucked a boy. Our station director, Mike Wales, knew them both and had even referred them from time to time. He thought of it as a service for special clients who needed some 'particular' action; I thought of it as pimping pure and simple, but why would I give a shit? I didn't.

Mike was completely straight, but a solid realist. Sex, drugs and rock-n-roll; nothing bothered him as long as it fell within his 'live and let live' philosophy. He'd served in 'Nam, but was pretty well adjusted despite the experience. Some of the others around the terminal most definitely were not; they called it shell-shock. 'Post-Traumatic Stress Disorder' was a phrase not yet coined but we sure as hell knew all about it. Mike would almost invariably take the side of the underdog in *any* kind of conflict. He was always stable and fair in his dealings; but if he thought a 'superior,' be it a boss, foreman, supervisor, cop or whatever, was abusing someone by dint of their position, it would unleash a side of him you damn well did not want to experience a second time.

Standing at my office though, a sort of glassed booth central to the loading docks and terminal aprons, I could see about half the facility and people at any one time. To the left were the fuel islands, to the right the docks, in the far distance directly in front was a major parking area, and the booth backed up to the main building, with the restaurant, supply shop, service center, offices and facilities. If you were going to hang out at a truck stop and wanted to see it all, take your pick, there was hardly a better place to be.

"Hey Matt, take these out to that Schultz driver was just in here," Mike told me as he handed me a clipboard. Rumpled sheets of white, pink and yellow flimsies smeared by greasy hands flapped on it. "Get him to sign off the A and D sheets and come on back." I was on my fifth (and last) morning of 'training.' I already had the whole drill down cold, and Mike knew it; this was the first he'd actually checked on what I was doing since Tuesday. He shoved another pile of clipboards and paperwork to 'my' side of the counter, then headed back up to his office in the main building.

Walking out to the truck lot I waved at a couple of drivers sitting in their rigs. Two seemed to watch me a bit closer than the others, their gazes following me as I passed. One in particular; he grinned and leered, then gave a thumbs-up sign. He wore a black cap, and his dark eyes glinted above a thick goatee and 'stache in his bright cab. I waved back, then spotted the nasty old Schultz trailer two rows across from him. I quickly zigged across the lot to over it.

Climbing up to the driver's side window, I rapped 3 or 4 times to rouse the driver from his sleeper. He came to the window in his boxers, and groggily accepted the clipboard, signed where I told him and headed back to his bunk. I considered taking a longer route to walk back to the station office, but retraced my steps past that nice white truck with the dark, handsome driver.

I deliberately made my path run closer to his rig, and he spotted me as soon as I came around the truck ahead of his. He had his window open before I came alongside the door, and called down.

"Hey! You're the new office guy, right? Chuck here!"

I grinned and answered, "Matt! Nice to meet ya, Chuck."

"You too; man it's a nice day! Maybe you wanna come sit up here and have a Coke with me? Take it easy for a spell huh?"

The simplicity of the come-on was beautiful: it was crystal-clear what he was inviting me up there for, but also utterly innocent. Take it or leave it; it should always be so easy. Of course I opted to take it... why wouldn't I?

I got to the passenger side and clambered up into the rig. Closing the door, I noticed he was turned in his chair to face me as much as he could. He already gripped a fairly prominent bulge in his jeans. He grinned as I got into the seat.

"Yeah buddy! I was hopin' I'd get a chance to meet you up close. You need something to drink, or maybe just wanna get to it?"

"Well, I don't really need a soda; what is it you wanna 'get to' anyhow?"

"Um, well... to be honest I'd really just like you to wrap those pretty lips around my dick and take a load off me. But if you wanna get off too, I'll take care of you."

"Hell yeah man, I'll suck you off... we can 69."

"Fine!" He quickly got up and moved to the bunk of the sleeper. His shirt was quickly off and dropping his jeans I looked admiringly at his furry body. It wasn't as thick as the fur of his goatee, but dark, <u>long</u> hairs made it luxuriant. I swiftly moved to kneel between his legs as he sat on the edge of the bunk. I opened my work pants and pulled my cock from behind my jockstrap as I simply leaned forward and sucked him in, burying my nose in the thick fur.

I intended to join him up on the bunk, but he leaned back as I began to give him head and I stroked my own hard cock. I would've liked to 69 and watch my cock sliding in and out of his bearded face, but I was, ahem, *busy...*

"Yeah, yeah buddy, suck that dick man! Oh god yeah take it in!" Hot and hard, his cock was a bit more than 6 inches and uncut. I moved up and down and the totality of the situation had me rock-hard in seconds. *I was sucking a trucker!* Doing the parking lot, *while on the job!* Oh I was 'on the job' all right; more like 'on the knob' as I sucked up and down and then gripped his cock with my free hand.

I stroked his shaft up and down, then tugged a bit more firmly and slid his foreskin completely back from his cockhead. He groaned and swiveled his hips, then leaned back again. I'd only sucked uncut dicks a couple times, even though I'd known more than a few uncut men in school and on the swim team. I knew about head cheese, smegma, but thank god this one was wonderfully clean. The unique scent of his foreskin sent waves of pleasure into my sinuses as he groaned again, enjoying his blow-job.

"Fuck yeah buddy, oh god yeah get it for me man, shit!"

Reaching up between his legs, I cupped his balls snugly as I slurped up and down his thick rod. Allowing his foreskin to slip back over his cockhead, I'd push his tool all the way back into my tonsils, then gently tug the skin of his whole shaft back down, allowing that sensitive cockhead to pop out while buried in my throat. It sent Chuck into spasms.

"Oh fuck yeah fuckin' damn buddy! Yeah man, you're good! Oh hell yeah!" he groaned. I drooled more and it moistened his crotch-pelt, making him just that much more fragrant. My own cock oozed and between feeling his furred legs and hairy balls I was reaching down to jack and stroke myself.

"Jeez, Matt, you're getting' me close buddy, oh god yeah! Go buddy, suck me!"

All I could do was make slurping noises like *fleeblemummmph* and *glurrrbblggggh...* and felt my own cock swelling in heat from the sheer horny lust of the moment. I reached up and down his furry legs, stroked up his chest and gripped a nipple as I neared climax. Once more I pulled his 'skin down as I jammed that super-sensitive dickhead between my tonsils. The timing couldn't have been better.

"Oh god man, suck that cock oh yeah! Fuck yeah buddy I'm gonna cum, I'm gonna cum, here ya go I'm gonna CUM!" he moaned, then thrust his pelvis upward. His hands grabbed the back of my head and held me impaled on his dick as my own load spurted out against his jeans, the edge of the bunk, onto my hand... I think I sprayed everything below the two-foot line in that sleeper as I knelt on the floor sucking my very first trucker-cock.

As I felt my own sticky white semen pumping out, my mouth was taking spurt after hot, salty spurt from the furry man fucking my face. He ground himself up once again, then released my head just as I thought I would choke. I pulled away and gasped for air, leaving a beautifully thick, obscene strand of his sperm stretching from his cockhead into my mouth. I got a breath and quickly began to savor, to slosh that thick cum around on my tongue.

"Oh fuck yeah, man!" he said, as I gulped and enjoyed it. "Fuck yeah!" He relaxed a moment as I returned to sucking his cock very gently, making sure I missed no morsels of the manly goodness.

After a long moment, he reached beneath my armpits and pulled me upward.

"Here buddy, c'mon. Need some help?" His fat, uncut cock flopped upward on his body, pasted into the thick fur, his 'skin still rolled back and his bared cockhead glowing bright red.

I chuckled a bit sheepishly. "Nah... actually I don't." He looked at me questioningly.

"I was jackin' while you were buckin' and fuckin' my face. I shot my wad too."

He laughed with me. "Cool! That's fine! I'll do ya if I gotta, ya know... anytime! But it's OK with me if I don't gotta!"

That attitude isn't all that uncommon, but especially true among truckers I came to learn. The guy was married, really another str8 boy at heart... but he liked a good blow job, and women can't suck dick. He liked blow jobs enough that he was willing to enjoy giving one in order to enjoy receiving one; quite amicable, really! But it was fine as it was. I assured him I'd do him again, and take him up on his offer to share next time.

We buttoned up quickly, neither ashamed nor hurried, but our connection was done. He really didn't want company, and I really didn't care to hang out with him. But dang! That uncut dick and his hot cum sure was a nice treat in the mid-morning.

"OK Matt, that sounds great! See ya again soon!" he called as I was moving to the door.

I clambered back out and down. "Later Chuck! Next time, buddy!"

Once more he gave me a thumbs-up as I headed back to the office, my first truck encounter completed. There would be many more, we all knew that already!

MEMORIAL WEEKEND

My 4th week on the job was Memorial Weekend, and I came in early. I knew that Doug, the night supervisor, would leave me a wad of paperwork to sort through. I flatly refused to do it for fat Greg or sleazy Darryl, the other supervisors. But Doug had told me directly that he had a terrible time reading: it was a major difficulty for him and he struggled mightily at those tasks. Plus, he had offered to do any thing, any time for me if I would undertake to double-check his paperwork.

Doug was very attractive, sandy hair and a well-muscled body despite something of a tummy. He was about 37 and carried a most enticing and substantial bulge in his Roebuck's work pants; but 'anything' hadn't meant sex. Furthermore, I didn't think screwing around with a coworker was the best idea. The truckers and day laborers came and went; Doug was a long-term employee.

I entered the booth and sat on the high stool. The counter along the front window ran from one side of the booth to the other, the intercom, fuel controls, a light panel showing which bays were occupied, and the bills-of-lading were all mixed in with the various detritus of a transit and fuel station counter. Doug was out on the apron talking to a big bearded beer-bellied guy, getting him ready to haul a load of Minnesota timber out of the place. He waved as I began to sift through the night's receipts.

From behind the flatbed with the timber a tall driver in a blue baseball cap walked up to them, then motioned and came towards the booth. He looked to be about 30, with medium brown hair and a thick moustache. Nice golden eyes twinkled in his tanned face, his slim frame belied the mass of manly flesh pushing at the front of faded denim jeans. A *large* mass...

He stuck his head in the doorway and smiled, then offered a hand. "Hey bud, how ya doing?" The Tennessee twang was nice, soft and Confederate. I was kind of 'smitten' in an instant. I shook his hand and felt the sinews of well-formed farm muscles in there; the rest of him was no doubt just that much finer.

"Howdy there. What can I do for you this morning?"

"Well I got some trouble here my friend. That driver is kinda fucked up and I can't use him for this run. We gotta head to damn Tucson and he ain't gonna last. Shit, I don't think he'll last to Hennepin Avenue." The Belly-Boy looked fucked up alright... he was in bad shape. Drunk at 6:07 AM wasn't good.

"Yeah? How can I help? I can move a truck around but I sure ain't licensed for OTR hauling..." My voice had instantly picked up a hint of his accent.

"No buddy, I didn't mean that! Hehehe... I ain't asking you to join me! But..." Maybe he was thinking about how teaming with me *would* go? His keys hung on his right hip belt loop; if that was a signal, he liked to get fucked. And damn, I would not at all mind fucking him, either. At all. He chuckled again and there was a slight but distinct pulsation in my cock. (*Throbb*...)

"But I have to wait here at least another 18 hours, maybe even till tomorrow for a replacement. We're contract teamed; I can't grab a lone wolf and just go. I'm going to have to stow it for at least 18 hours... or longer. Even open ended, you know?"

"Of course. There's the whole damn lot, buddy, pick a slot!"

"Um, that's the trouble. This jerk at the mill up in Duluth supervised loading, and that trailer is so lopsided if I try to haul into your lot down there I think I'll damn well roll it over." He paused, let out a slow breath. My dick pulsed again, thickening noticeably. I shifted my weight to loosen the tension in there as it was bent over in my jockstrap and couldn't stretch out. Another minute and my growing hard-on would be painful.

"When a replacement gets here, we can adjust the stacks. And I can't do THAT alone either, and Company regulations say forklifting has to be our guys, so I can't get the yardbirds to help. I need to stay on the apron and park..."

(God he smelled good, a clean scent of masculine aroma, *pheromones* to the nth degree. No wonder my body was reacting to him so early in the day! I wasn't sure if it was his pits, crotch, hair or asshole I was smelling. All the above no doubt.)

I continued for him, "And that means you're going to be stuck there in the middle of my loading turn the whole fucking day." He nodded sheepishly. My tone was a bit harsh, not insolent but 'hassled,' as if it was *really* going to put me out. He knew it was a matter of course in operations, but beyond normal. He 'owed me' one. He'd have to make it up somehow...

I smacked him on the shoulder. "Yeah I gotcha cowboy. Come out here and I'll show ya." I intended to find a spot beside the mechanical shops and make someone move for him... impress him with my authority.

The pressure in my jock was too much though, and I had to adjust. Dan's eyes widened as I groped myself through the front of my blue work pants to loosen up, then quickly he looked away. But he recovered himself just as quickly, and didn't realize I'd caught him looking.

He grinned and straightened himself up. Dang he was nice and tall, taller than me. He had to be 6'5 and in boots more like 6'9... and at 180 pounds or so I figured his jeans to be size 30 x 36. He turned to go out the door and I got a good view of the back of him. Goddam, that soft denim looked like it had been spray-painted on his ass. Snug, form fitting, beautiful. The line along the lower edges of his round orbs told me either tight Jockeys or even better, a nice, sung *jockstrap* was in there. His keys jangled as he walked. I followed him out the door and then moved around him to go check out the truck and show him a safe idling spot.

I made small talk; I just wanted to hear more of that laconic voice. "Tucson, huh? I've ridden through there, kinda nice in the desert."

He grunted. "Yeah bud! I like getting out in that part of the country. Can getcherseff lost out there and love every second of it. Roadrunner territory!"

"For sure bubba, for sure. I went alone last time; woulda been a lot nicer with a buddy to share it." I let the idea trail off. By now I was sure he'd know exactly what I meant.

"Man hell yeah," he said softly. "Last time, a stop in Yuma, I took the tent out into the hills and stayed the night. Alone. The sunset didn't go down till almost 10:00. Goddam I wished someone coulda seen that with me..." I grunted softly, total assent. He glanced sidelong at me, carefully, self-consciously. From the bravadoccio of an OTR trucker, he was suddenly almost painfully shy. I knew in an instant it was a facet of him few, *very* few people ever got to see.

We got up to the truck where Mr. Belly was still standing with Doug. Damn he was a mess. More than 100 pounds over-weight, wheezing and pock-marked, he had all the traits of a hardcore hillbilly trucker. I bet in his day he was a good one, but now he was way past prime. He smiled wanly at the driver, then spoke in that thick Southern-trucker-ese.

"Hey Danny, you get us set with the office man here?" He was almost heaving to talk, I was deeply concerned. He looked to be in about the same shape my German professor, Dr. Hilgendorf, had been moments before he collapsed with a devastating and ultimately fatal stroke. He wasn't drunk, he was damn near ready to drop. Danny was getting worried too.

"Yeah George, I got it square. I think you gonn' hafta take it easy a spell here buddy." George nodded.

"I just needs mah pills. I done forgitt 'em ya know."

"What pills you talkin' about?" I asked, almost sharply. He knew I meant to have an answer, too.

He looked at me quizzically. He was not used to anyone giving a shit; suddenly that fine Danny and now me were concerned enough to pry into what he thought was personal stuff, the medical stuff.

"Um... I cain't say it. It's one of them *pree*-scription thangs the sawbones done gived me. They's blue, thats all I know. But I get sorry lightheaded and stuffy when I don't got 'em."

I nodded. "I know exactly what they are, George. You gonn' be in real trouble here in a minute. Now Danny, you take this boy back into the coffee house there and set with him. I'm gonn' make a call to someone I know."

"Um buddy... the truck is..."

I cut him off. "You leave that shit right where it is; that's my worry. Doug, I'm gonn' need you to stay in here a bit longer. Tell anyone who don't like it that that lumberyard is <u>stayin'</u> right there until the *yard supervisor* moves it. Got it?" He nodded. "Now you boys just go over in there and set till I come get you. And <u>don't</u> drink any more goddam coffee!"

Danny, probably 10 or 12 years my senior and George, 30 years more than that, complied as though I was their school-teacher. Dan began to lead George away and looked back at me. "It's Matthew," I said, and he smiled brightly.

I headed back into the booth as Doug went onto the aprons to oversee the outgoing freighters. Quickly I telephoned a friend of my folks', a doctor, and told her of George. I hung up and began to clear my paperwork while I waited.

In less than 15 minutes a dark blue Cadillac pulled up at the side of the control booth. Dr. Lillian MacKenzie, a nationally-known surgeon and (oh god, don't tell the truckers THIS!) gynecologist stepped out and motioned to me. In a flash I was out there to talk to her. Quickly I explained my feelings and 'diagnosis,' and she told me to take her into the coffee shop. She grabbed one of those honest-to-God little black doctor bags from her car and we headed into the building.

She looked George over quickly, then pulled the cuff from her bag. Making a fast, basic exam, she then turned to me and whispered, "This man is going to die if he doesn't get into Arapaho," meaning the nearby hospital where she practiced. "You spotted the most serious case of hypertension I've ever seen in someone still standing." George did not want to get into an ambulance, his fear and pride regarding being stretchered out of the truck stop was apparent. Even Dr. MacKenzie, for all her feminist power trip, acquiesced and offered to take him herself. He was still unconvinced.

"Now George, you gonna go with Dr. Lillian here and take a ride in her *COOP DAY-VILL*," I insisted. "It's just up the street a short piece and they'll get you all patched up. You be back here in time for lunch, OK?" He still looked a bit scared, but the idea of riding in her fine Cadillac had him; I doubted he'd ever sat in such a car in his 60+ years. They rose from the table and we escorted them out to her car. Danny and I watched as they pulled away.

He reached to my shoulder and squeezed lightly. "Matthew... Matt? That was a fine thing you done. I been worried about him for the last couple days. I didn't know what to do..." I reached to him and put my hand on his body, right above his belt, just a reassuring stroke.

"Did what I thought needed done is all. He gonn' be OK buddy."

Danny smiled, and we returned to the booth. Doug had gotten the traffic lined up and things were running smoothly. But he was almost 2 hours past punching out and I told him to get gone. He smacked me on the back and said, "Whatever you say Doc! See you tomorrow!" The nickname stuck from that moment on.

The Tennessee trucker wandered around the facility most of the day, bored and listless. But he got us a Coke and chatted with me while I ran the shop. He popped in right on the dot of noon with a burger and fries, and we had lunch together. The more time we were in the same room, the more we were heating each other up. That unspoken connection became stronger and stronger. He never said, "Wanna come out to the truck with me?" and I never said, "We'll need to get a room so I can fuck you." But we both knew damn well as soon as I could punch the time clock we'd be heading someplace private. Very private...

When we finished lunch, I opened up a parking slot beside the mechanic's shop and told Dan to move his cluster-fuck-truck around the building and into it. I hauled myself up into the cab with him and directed him around the buildings and across the acres of pavement. He smelled wonderful, the sleeper of the cab beckoning us both, but we knew we'd have to wait a bit longer. He pulled up where I told him and parked. I grunted a compliment, and was going to get out, back to work. Dan was staring straight ahead and didn't look at me.

"You going to spend the day here? Just hang out in the cab?" I asked him. He looked wistful, preoccupied.

"I want... I wanna... I don't want... don't want you to... oh fuck, *I don't know!."* I thought he was going to cry.

I reached over to him and grabbed his shoulder. Finally he turned to me and the desire, the hot passion and wanting, the painful *wanting* in his eyes almost scared me. He tried to smile.

"Danny..." I had to stand up to move across the center area of the cab, but I climbed over him and pushed him back on his chair. Straddling his body, I wrapped my arms around him and leaned in close, tight. My breath was hot on him, and as I made contact in that first kiss it was as if he melted, literally melted in my arms. He sucked me into him, kissing and holding me, moaning softly.

It was a long 20 seconds or so; it just seemed to go on and on. Finally though, I broke the kiss and pulled back from him. I smiled.

"That's just a teaser," I said. "There's a <u>lot</u> more where that came from, OK?"

The bulge in his jeans was prominent, tight and huge. I stroked across the front of them slowly, feeling the hot meat beneath. He squirmed, moaned again.

"Oh god Matt... man, we have to spend the night together, OK?"

"Jeez, Dan... there's no way in heaven or hell I'm going anywhere but into that sleeper with you buddy. The <u>minute</u> I get done with my shift I'm going to rip those clothes off you man."

He smiled widely, a great relieved grin. "Yeah! OK! I'll be here man... I'll wait. How long though?"

"Shit dude, it's past one now; I finish at <u>two</u>!"

Again the relief was palpable. Suddenly his whole body relaxed and a world of taut anxiety I didn't know was there suddenly dissipated. "Oh man..."

"Yeah. All I gotta do is go over the log sheets and get that ready. Fat Greg will be here and he's always on time. Make it all his problem!"

We laughed and I got off his lap. But not before I sank my tongue into his mouth once more for a long slow kiss. He held me tight, grinding his crotch up against mine. The promise of beauty and pleasure to come... He ground himself harder, slowly writhing in my embrace, then arched up and held me tight. At last we broke the embrace.

I was ready to climb out of the truck. "You going to stay up here alone, or come screw around while I finish my shift?"

"Well, I don't think I should go out there like this..." He motioned to the front of his jeans. A large wet spot stained the faded material a dark, obvious color.

"Damn man! You oozing that much? I am too, but shit!"

"No Matt, it's not oozing. You made me cum."

"Aw man..." I reached to stroke that bulge again, thinking I should rip those jeans open and take a taste of his cock, his load. But I stopped.

"Keep those clothes on, OK? I want to undress you myself when I get back, real nice and slow. Wait for me! OK?"

"Fuck yeah man, yeah... OK. Hurry back, alright?"

"Two o'clock buddy. On the dot." I badly wanted to kiss him once more, but I opened the door and hopped out of the truck before the heat of that moment made me do something I might regret.

"LET ME"

I was all but incapable of dealing with the mundane paperwork scattered on the counter. I stacked up a handful of the freight logs and shoved them into a drawer. Greg would never go looking for them and if he did come across them he sure wouldn't do anything about it. I'd get to them in the morning.

Three minutes before 2:00 he came screeching into the car lot, his souped-up, filthy Camaro rocking into his customary place. A fast-food soda cup fell from the door as he hauled his blubbery ass out and sauntered up to the booth. He looked around, sizing it up. Most everything was neat, he was satisfied.

"Hey."

"Hey Greg. Nothing to worry about, except we got a Superior Lumber trailer on a Chattanooga Lines hauler behind the garage. Fucked up load, no second driver."

He grunted. "How long?"

"Till he leaves."

"OK. Don't need that strip back there anyhow."

"Yeah that's why I put him out there. And there's still the spot behind him even if you do get another idler like him."

"Gotcha."

Greg was a slob and would be just as lazy as you let him, but he knew what he was doing. I grabbed my jacket and headed for the office to punch out. He probably wouldn't notice or care, but I didn't want him to see me go back behind the garage to Danny's rig. I'd head out the back doors from the office.

I hustled through the station and into the office. A fast grab and clack, my card was punched and I was done. I doubted the fat cunts in there even noticed I'd been through. So much the better. Around the corner, out the door and 20 yards down the pavement, up the step and I pulled the door open on the truck with the TN plates. Danny was still in the driver's seat; somehow I knew he hadn't moved since I'd left. I clambered up and in, yanking the door closed behind me.

He smiled as if in relief, maybe he didn't believe I was coming back? No way I was passing up the chance with him though. He was trying to haul himself up to greet me as I threw myself onto his lap and pushed him back into the chair. With nary a sound but low grunts of pure horny pleasure we clasped into a tight, hot embrace, locked instantly into a wet, deep kiss. Again, and again. Nothing was spoken but we kissed and began to paw and stroke one another. Finally, with my cock straining in my pants, bent over hard and oozing, I pulled back and looked at this man. Once more I thought perhaps he was near tears.

I stroked the side of his face, his chin and moustache. I touched the corner of his eye and he kissed my fingertip as it brushed past his mouth. "*Mmmmmmmm!*"

I pulled off of him to let him up. The cab was not quite high enough for men our height to stand, but it was close. The rear compartment was taller, but on the bed-deck we wouldn't be standing up much anyhow.

Dan reached into the side compartment and pulled a neat stack of cloth from the shelf.

He unfolded the stack, and with shaking hands began to curtain off the windows. It took rather longer than you'd expect, he was a bit rattled. But I said nothing and let him make his hospitality preparations. Finally we were alone, in a private little cave. A snug retreat where nothing of the world could find us. I pulled him towards me again, and kissed him slowly, tight and hot.

We turned and I pulled him with me as I sank onto the lower berth. Sliding back, I was on the bed, then turned him onto his back, laying beneath me as I pressed against his body and kissed him again and again. My hands roamed down the front of him, his chest, his arms and face, his body, his crotch. The bulge of his manhood was hot and firm, his Levi's still very damp from the inadvertent load he'd shot while we made out an hour earlier.

I stroked him as he tugged at my shirt, the waistband of my work pants. My cock throbbed, oozing in my strap. I took hold of his forearm and stopped him.

"*Let me...*" I whispered.

He relaxed, again almost melting as I took over. He wanted, expected, rejoiced in it that I took control of him and began to unbutton his shirt. His golden eyes sparkled as I opened the front, then slid the cloth off him. He lifted his torso up to let me pull it away and cast it aside. Then his blue T-shirt... I tugged the buckle of his belt open. He gasped slightly as I once more brushed firmly onto his basket. His keys rattled and I lay onto him, my hand gripping the top of his waistband, fingers *juuuuuuust* going into his jeans, behind the elastic of his strap. I kissed him again. I nuzzled onto his neck and nipped him, the manly scent making me heady with lust.

I stroked him from face to feet as I moved over him, then yanked the laces of his boots. One... two... then off. I pulled his socks off and lifted his foot to my mouth. I kissed the top of one foot, then licked his toes. He groaned, gasped and wriggled them as I ran my hand up the inside of his leg, onto his warm, moist thigh.

Raising up onto my knees, I then finished unbuttoning my own shirt, then threw it with the pile of Danny's clothes on the floor. I stripped off my undershirt, then undid my belt, tugging it out from the carriers and tossing it aside. My work pants open and unzipped, the wide white band of my jockstrap topping the edge of the pouch below... he reached up and lightly pawed my belly. This time I grunted and flexed; then quickly pulled off my own boots and socks.

I stretched my body the full length of his, not letting my weight rest upon him but holding myself up from the deck, and leaned down to kiss his wet mouth again. He raised his arms up, laying back with his hands to the sides of his head, open, vulnerable, waiting. I sucked his tongue and slobbered into his mouth, probing with my own.

Letting my left arm relax, I sank beside him, longways. Finally I could reach the rest of him with ease and took hold of the band of his jeans. He lifted his hips to let me slide them down... down... and off. He lay in glorious tan, his bulge cupped in the pouch of a slightly frazzled jockstrap, moist with thick drying cum. His nicely muscled chest was smooth and defined, his nipples stark and erect, hot, sensitive. I slowly maneuvered his Levi's behind me and dropped them, then slid the curtain of the sleeper deck closed, a further barrier to the world outside. We were in an 8 x 5' den, alone, the only two men on earth.

My hand slowly ran up the inside of his thigh, from his knee to his secret area, and slowly stroked over his jock. His cock jumped within, then poked the head out from the side. Easily he was 8½", closer to 9. His balls were snug in the knit pouch and I cupped them in my hand as again I pressed my mouth over his. Our breaths came in short hot gasps, raspy and quick. Words were superfluous, we said nothing.

Danny reached into the accessory bin mounted on the bulkhead and brought out a white container, 2" round thing. I surmised it to be lube, and the small brown bottle was obvious. He handed the gear to me, his eyes saying, *Do as you will... take me.*

I set the things beside him and at last began to slide out of my blue work pants. Danny's eyes followed every move, taking in the sight as I exposed my own muscley chest to him, the light dusting of fur leading into my jockstrap, the outline of my big dick pushing the pouch outward. He touched me lightly as I moved him and positioned myself between his outstretched legs. A trail of sweat ran down the center of my chest, through the fine hair. Again he raised his arms, laying back, open and inviting.

His knees turned outward and I knelt between them, then pawed the tan smooth legs. Running my hand up his thigh, I finally reached the bulging jock and let my fingers seek the area beneath, down, down... down to his hot asshole. He squirmed and ground his hips a bit, moaning almost inaudibly. I lifted one leg, then the other. He spread them for me, expecting me to get into the saddle. I lifted them higher, farther apart, then ran my tongue from his knee downward, and sank into a crouching heap between his legs.

Pushing him upward, I licked and nipped, bit and chewed his thighs as his gasps became more and more pronounced. My hands behind his knees, I forced him backward and open, then slowly sank my face onto the pouch of his jock, sniffing in the aroma, becoming drunk and all but insane with lust. I slobbered and licked, sucked against the fabric, feeling the full hot hardness of his shaft behind the elastic, his oozing cockhead sticking out the side. My body was taut, hot and straining as I controlled myself to move slowly, carefully and sensuously on the man beneath me.

With a slow suction, I traveled up the length of his dick and finally, finally took him into my mouth. He groaned, grunted as his hard meat sprang upward, pulsing even harder as I sucked him in. Slowly I let my face slide up and down, taking him from the tip of his dick to the depths of his fragrant, soft bush. With a slight force as I sucked his cock, the strap slipped aside and his balls fell free, hanging down between his hot thighs.

I sucked him a moment longer, then let his dick slip out of my mouth. Licking my way down the underside of his tube, I wet his bush, then his balls. I slurped and took first one, then the other into my hungry mouth. Then sucking harder; I pushed the side of his sac up and took them both into the wet warmth, tonguing his loose skin and letting them roll within my mouth.

He ground his pelvis forward, letting out a hot gasp of sensation. "Oh!" He moaned again and let me continue, trying to spread his legs farther, lifting them high. Again pushing him backward I sank onto him, and let my tongue slide down the base of his cock to his asshole. A flick of the tongue, then a slurp, then...

I buried my face into the short tight split of his crack, and chewed on his hole with slobbering heat.

Quickly adjusting my position, I held his butt cheeks in both hands, pulling the flesh open to allow me total access, totally exposing his most private spot to my lusty invasion. He gasped and began a low moaning, groaning that continued from then on.

I ate him out for minutes, sliding my tongue into him, licking and chewing on his pucker, kneading his butt cheeks and the backs of his rump. Danny squirmed and pushed, trying to open himself wider, trying to let me farther and farther into him with my tongue, my breath, my fingers. I pulled back and stroked his hole and gently probed him. He grunted again and puckered, then relaxed. My finger slid into him to the knuckle, then fully. I turned my hand this way, then that, then retreated. I let his legs droop and drop back down as I rose to kiss him

The scent of his hot manly asshole covered my face and moustache as we once more coupled our mouths. He didn't flinch a bit as I kissed him, wet and sloppy with the moisture of my rimming. The taste of his own anus excited him even more, and he groped my back, pulling me onto him and lifting his legs, wrapping them around me.

I reached for the poppers and twisted the cap, then took a slow medium hit. I offered them back to him and he took one in each nostril, then leaned back sailing in my embrace. I reached then for the lube and flipped the small container open, dipping into the white cream.

With a fingerful of Elbow-Grease I reached between his legs, beneath the pouch of his sweaty jock and found his opening. Sliding the grease onto him and into him, I probed and lubed him, then got another dollop. I raised myself up and let my cock flop out the side of my now damp jockstrap and stroked myself, greasing and lubing my cock. Dan's eyes followed my every move in pure lust, pure desire as I prepared to enter him.

Lifting his legs high and wide, I propped them up on my shoulders and positioned myself at his opening. My cockhead touched the puckering hole and he flexed, then relaxed. His eyes closed slowly as he awaited the feeling of my manly tool opening his body. With a slow steady pressure I began to enter, and slid about 2" of my dick into the tight ring of his sphincter.

His eyes clenched tightly closed, I guessed it was intense, perhaps painful and I slowed. Leaning forward I pulled his shoulders from behind and lifted him up to kiss him. He clamped tightly onto my kiss but kept his eyes closed fast. Again I pressed forward and the next 2" slid into his ass, opening him past the ring and sliding my oozing cockhead into his rectum. He gasped, his hands clenching at my butt, holding me back, yet pulling me forward. He would not protest, I knew, yet I was determined not to hurt him. I paused, I kissed him and backed away, taking my cock from within him.

His eyes opened, fluttered as if he was being rejected, but I didn't give him time for the thought. Handing him the poppers again, I dipped another glob of grease from the white tub and slipped it onto his asshole as he hit the bottle. He leaned back, the rush taking him and I took a deep huff as well. I quickly greased my cock again, then resumed. The amyl did its job and with a slow but full push I was in him to the hilt, and he spread himself wide and willing, pulling me down onto himself in a hot tight embrace. We kissed and I held him fast.

He ground against me, then began a hot low moan. He grunted, tried to push his hips upward with his cock burrowed against my body. I rose slightly, his cock jumping up as I held him, not moving my dick in his tunnel at all. Yet his body, overwhelmed in the sensations and his own needs, went over the edge and his piss-slit flared open, oozed and spurted the first thick gobs of Danny's cum onto us both. He bucked, gritted his teeth and shot again, then again. I watched in honor and fascination as he came, giving me his most precious semen. In a second I was with him, my own lust boiling over and I shot my load hot and deep, pouring 5 full spurts of cum into him. I groaned quietly, low and full, as my balls split asunder and dumped themselves into his willing body.

Coupled in that hot mass of flesh, I simply held him as we floated and sailed in our orgasm. At long last his eyes opened and he focused on me. A slow smile spread across his face as I began to deflate within the warm confines of his ass. Relaxing, I let his legs slide down and released him slowly, my dick slipping out of him in silence. Once more I kissed him, then rolled onto the mat beside him.

I cradled his body, his shoulders and head against my arm. My hand absentmindedly stroked up his leg, back into that hot sweaty area under his basket. I fingered his hole and felt a gob of my load ooze out onto my hand. I brought it up slowly, laid it on the fur of my moustache as had been done to me and then leaned in to kiss him. We slurped and shared it. Slowly I laid him back as his eyes closed in sensuous relief.

We lay a long moment like that, and as his breathing became slow and rhythmic I realized he'd fallen asleep. His peaceful face nestled near my armpit, I held him, letting him float in the peace after our beautiful fucking. I closed my eyes for a bit too, and just held him close.

SHOWER TIME

Danny nestled in my arms for half an hour or so. I think I dozed a bit too, but I was looking into his fine features when his eyes slowly opened. He smiled, focused and the hugged me snugly. My arm had long since gone into numbness, but I hadn't moved it lest I disturb the beautiful reverie Danny was floating in. He woke fully, then began to move next to me.

It wasn't until he spoke that I clearly realized we had had no words, no talking or verbal encouragement at all while we fucked. Just pure man-lust, moans and slurping and bodily sensations, the unspoken knowledge of what the other wanted and needed. Then, that mind-numbing powerful climax.

"Ummmm... you're still here..."

I smiled, kissed him again. "Of course I am Dan. I wouldn't run off after *that*... Besides, you said you wanted me to spend the night with you. Would you rather I didn't?"

His eyes flickered and he started up. "Oh no! Please no! I really do want you to stay Matt, please? Stay with me?"

Now it was my turn to relax. I exhaled and smiled back. "*Yeah*, oh yeah Dan! OK... I want to hold you all night, wake up in the morning like we just did."

I shifted to free my arm and our private den creaked, suddenly reminding me we were in a truck after all. I wanted a smoke, and began to reach for my clothes. Danny was sitting up also. He looked down at himself, the limp and soggy bulge of his jock, the rubbery mass of cum pasted on his belly, on me. His cum. He slowly reached to it, ran a finger through it and lifted it up.

Taking hold, I pulled his wrist and hand toward me, then drew that finger into my mouth, looking at Danny's wondering face as I did. Slurping the thick gob off his finger, I then released his hand and leaned in to share his juice with him, from my tongue. We kissed, swapping it back and forth. He was in ecstasies again.

"God... you made me cum without even touching my dick! I barely remember it though... I... umm... well I remember it, but..."

"Hey, it's OK! I know what you mean. Kind of a haze huh?"

"Yeah, *that's* it. Hazy, but so nice... just so nice..." He paused, introspective and moot. "You made me cum twice. I ain't done anything for you have I?"

"HUH? Danny... man... I blew my load like a damn cannon buddy."

"You did?"

"It's inside you, my juice is up inside you man. I cummed when you did."

He smiled, once more relieved. "Wow, yeah... yeah, OK." His hand once more ran down his body, to his crotch, below... I put my hand on the back of his.

"Yeah buddy, yeah..." He squirmed slightly, parting his legs enough for me to slide a finger into his asshole. I drew out a gob of my own load, a *big* gob, and held it up for us both to admire. As before, I laid my finger across my upper lip and smeared it across my mouth. I leaned forward, my lips parted, ready.

"Oh yeah Matt... yes. Oh god man, *yes*," and he leaned up to me, his eyes closing as we kissed and shared 'our' cum. I found the cigarettes in my shirt pocket and fished one out. Danny quickly reached up to the accessory bin and found a lighter. Striking expertly for me, he lit me up and laid snugly into my arm again. I exhaled.

"Ah yeah man, your smoke! Fine! So fine."

"You like one?"

"No man, I don't smoke. But I'm glad you do. Makes you look so hot. Well, makes *you* look that much hotter I think."

I smiled and took another drag, then handed it to him. He quickly took it and held it for me, as I began to sort out our garments. I motioned with my head, and he held it to my mouth and I pulled another drag. I put my clothes to our feet, his along the wall behind him.

He rustled a bit, then sat up. "I don't need to smoke, but I'm gonna need to piss real soon Matt." I nodded.

"Yeah me too. We can go upstairs, to the trucker's facility. It's only a bit after 3:00; there'll be hardly anyone up there." He smiled.

"I guess I should get dressed, get out of this messy jockstrap..."

"Danny, I wish you wouldn't. I saw that strap on you at 6:00 this morning, and swore I'd take it off you myself. And right now, *I don't want it off you*."

"You saw it? How?"

"The line on your ass. One of the many reasons I made sure we got this time together man."

He smiled and nodded. "Yeah, I like wearing it. I just about cummed when you got your pants off and I saw you was wearing one too."

My mind ran ahead. Jockstrap man; a beautiful (even if neurotic) big-dicked bottom man; ready to please, to go along with my wants and needs. Ready to comply... I thought of the showers upstairs. A private booth, him and me in hot water and steam... and jockstraps... and more. I was ready to indulge the obsessions further with him.

"Keep that strap on, and get your jeans, we're going upstairs man." He all but sprang into gear, it was obvious he liked me to tell him what to do. He needed someone in control.

Two or three minutes later we were dressed to go up, and climbed to the front of the cab. Danny stopped at the door before opening it, and looked at me. "What if someone's out there, what if someone sees us?"

I grunted. "Danny, I ain't ashamed of being with you. I'd be _proud_ if someone saw me getting out of here with you, and nobody, goddam _nobody_ is going to make me feel otherwise."

Dan's mind whirled and he closed his eyes. It was a thought he'd never entertained, that he could be anything but guilty with a guy he liked. He straightened up and opened the door. We clambered out and down to the pavement, and he stood tall and smiling as we walked to the back door of the building.

I lead him up the rear stairway to the "bath house," as they called it. Having my work keys on my belt (on the left, natch,) I let us into the facility through a staff door. Danny stayed at the end of the hallway while I went up behind the counter and grabbed a key to shower room #8, the last one on the hall. The attendant was watching TV 20 feet away from her desk. I held the key up and waved. She glanced up from

General Hospital just long enough to know an employee was in the area, but all 7 of the other keys were still on the board. We were alone up there.

I quickly returned, got Danny and opened the room. It was small, very cozy. Of course the shower rooms were intended for only one person at a time. Maybe five by seven feet, there was a tiled shower stall with a thick vinyl curtain, a changing area and a vanity-sink. There was no toilet.

We stepped inside and Dan looked about the room approvingly. I closed the door and once more swept him into my arms and kissed him. He grunted as I pressed him close. No doubt his bladder was beginning to give him powerful signals about impending bodily functions. I released him and said, "Strip."

He looked quizzically and began to undo his shirt, then his belt.

"What about...?" he started.

"Don't worry. Let's get naked."

I quickly got my boots and clothes off and stood in my jock; while Danny got the rest of his duds off I turned the shower on, hot. The steam began to fill the room. He got to his jockstrap and once more I had to stop him. "Leave that on."

He stood for a moment, then I stepped behind the curtain and into the shower stall. He followed and I adjusted the water, pointing the showerhead against the wall. We could stand in there close together, but not yet getting wet.

I pulled him close to me again, mashing my pouch against the front of his jock. My cock was thick, as was Dan's, and I slowly began to kiss him while holding him tightly. He responded, but obviously was concerned about his immediate need. Preoccupied.

I clamped my mouth upon his and my hand roamed down to his ass, then probed between his cheeks. My index finger found his hole and slowly began to enter. He squirmed in my embrace, but again tried to pull back. His cock was tight in the jockstrap, mashed up to mine. I held him tighter, but let him break the kiss.

"Matt... man, I gotta piss! I'm gonna go right now man! We gotta find a john."

"No we don't buddy. Let it go. Go. Right here. Right now."

His eyes widened, his mind raced. But he didn't try to pull away. I gripped his butt cheeks again, tight, holding him firmly. Then I felt around to the front, slipping my hand into the pouch of his strap, adjusting his hot cock so it was pointing upward, the pouch holding him snugly. The underside of my dick was pushed up against his, our faces close. I breathed into Danny's mouth, against his nose and whispered again, "Go. Do it..."

He held me as tight and closed his eyes. His lips parted and I felt his cock pulsate, his cock tube pressed to mine. It thickened, then filled. A slow warmth spread into my jock and the wetness grew. A second later we heard the splashing as the stream of his piss drained downward and hit the floor. Danny moaned, grunted, and let it flow.

"Ahhhhhh... oh wow. God Matt, wow..."

"Mmmm yeah Danny! That's it! Me too man!" I relaxed my muscles and in a second my piss began to flow and mingle with his. Holding each other in that tight embrace we pissed on and with each other. Dan ground himself onto my bulge, feeling the heat and enjoying the wetness. The heat of the shower made the scent of piss waft up, the pheromones sending us both back into horny lust.

I stopped my flow after just a few seconds, letting Danny drain as he needed. He slowed, then stopped. "Wow, yeah Matt! That's kinda hot!" I smiled, nodded.

"Yeah buddy, we're wet with it. No problem though, we can rinse off when we want to. Shower play is great." I stroked the front of his pouch, got my hand wet with piss and lifted it between us. I forced it to Dan's mouth before he had time to become queazy; once I smeared the piss onto his mouth and 'stache, I kissed him. He was astonished, but again didn't protest, nor try to break away.

"Mmmmm... mmmgmmph, yea... Oh damn! Fuck man! What are you DOING?"

"Tasting you man," I replied, "Tasting *us*. I want more, too." I loosened my grasp on him and slid to my knees. I tugged the front of his jockstrap and let it snap back onto his wet body. Then I pressed my face onto the hot pouch, licking and sucking from it. I chewed his cock, which thickened noticeably as I worked on him. Pulling the elastic side away, I let his cock flop out, wet and glistening. Slowly I took it into my mouth, slurping the piss from his shaft.

He groaned, thrusting his dick forward instinctively. The steam rose and he breathed heavily. I reached into the pile of our clothes and retrieved the poppers, and lifted them up to Danny. He accepted them slowly, opened the cap and took a deep hit, then another. I took them from his hand and snorted deeply myself.

"Relax buddy, relax. Let me have the rest..."

He swooned in the rush and closed his eyes. I took the head of his tool in my lips and waited. That fine cock pulsed gently, then a warm dribble flowed into my mouth. A spurt, then a slow stream. I slurped and tasted Danny, pawing at his belly while I drank him.

Again he moaned gently as he finished, drained. I sucked firmly, then slid down the whole length of his shaft, burying my nose in his fine soft bush. Then I rose, pulled Dan close onto my chest and kissed him again. He sucked my tongue, licked my moustache. The drips of piss on my face were intoxicating, he licked them all.

Leaning back and looking into his eyes I smiled, then put my hands onto his shoulders. I pressed on him and he began to sink down, then stopped. He looked at me quizzically, wondering.

"Yeah buddy, your turn. Try it man, you'll be amazed." He looked a bit frightened, worried about it. I ran my hand up his chest to his chin, then kissed him again.

"I didn't hurt you in the truck did I? Danny I won't hurt you now..." His expression brightened instantly, and he held my hips as he then sank onto the tile floor. He looked at the beautiful hump of flesh in my wet jockstrap, then slowly leaned forward and mashed his face onto the pouch. He sucked at the fabric, licked and slurped. I tugged it open as I'd done with his, and my fat dick popped free, standing straight out to his mouth.

Tentatively he extended his tongue, licking the slit of my dickhead. Slowly he opened his mouth and took me in. He sucked, taking half my length, then more. Gulping harder, he managed to get almost all of my throbbing organ into his gullet. I held his head and slowly face fucked him. Then I offered him the poppers again and as he took another huge hit, I turned the water temperature up a bit. The steam billowed around us, making it cloudy and hot. Taking the bottle back from him I hit deeply myself, once, twice, and gave it to him again. He hit twice more, I knew he was all but swooning.

As the rush reached its crescendo, I relaxed and pushed my cockhead between Dan's wet, quivering lips. I'd barely begun to piss while we were holding each other, so now... it flowed readily.

Dan didn't react much, but let the piss flow into his mouth and across his tongue. He must've stopped his glottis, as piss ran freely out from around my dick and flowed down his chin, his chest. His eyes were closed and he went with the rush. I stopped my pissing and pulled out; then leaned down to kiss him in my piss. He quickly joined me in the kiss, then I looked into his face and told him to relax, let it happen...

"Drink some buddy; taste it. Taste me. *Take my juice into you man*, like my cum is still deep up in your ass."

He smiled at that; it made total sense. He pursed his lips and took the head of my penis to the edge of the corona. I once more opened the valve and began to flow, slowly and softly. He let it fill his mouth, then gulped. Then again.

I pissed and he swallowed, then began to swivel around and grind while he nursed. His cock stood out from his jockstrap, straight, hot and <u>hard</u>. He made a low gurgling in his throat, I wondered if he was gagging, but the soft peace of his expression, his closed eyes told me it was pleasure. I pissed another hot stream, then it tapered off. One more short spurt, and I was done.

Danny suckled and slurped on my cock for a long moment longer, then opened his eyes. I reached under his armpits and tugged him to his feet. His smile told me of my success, and he was hot, ready for more.

I tugged his jock down, finally letting him remove it, then took mine off too. We tossed them out with our other clothes. Turning the showerhead into the stall, I held him and slathered soap up and down him, and bathed him. Then I told him to do me; he complied instantly. We cleaned off, kissing each other and stroking our cocks hard the whole time.

We finished and I turned the water off. The silence was deafening, and Dan looked at me as though we had been caught in public. I smiled and whispered to him.

"We're the only ones up here buddy, it's OK."

We stepped quietly out of the stall and began to dry off. My dick needed more, and Dan didn't notice as I pulled the Elbow Grease from my pants pocket. I turned him toward the vanity and pushed him forward, then slapped a gob of the grease on his already used hole. Slicking up my cock, I positioned behind him, then slowly but unstoppably forced myself up his ass.

Keeping his body leaned forward he grunted, moaned and huffed in pleasure. He arched his back and his head tilted backward. I wrapped my arms around his midsection and thrust upward again. He spread himself wider and I began to slide up and down, in and out of his hole with increasing heat. Humping and pummeling, I started to fuck him fast, hot and hard. I could see him grimace in the mirror, but he held the vanity edge tightly, standing solid and stable for my fucking.

I reached around and found his hard dick. My hand was still slick with Elbow and I stroked him fast and hard. My balls ached and swelled, my cock was throbbing with a double load of hot cum. The load I'd given him earlier was only a prelude, and now with the full action of hot *Fucking*, hot mansex with this strange guy, I just had that much more. I wanted, needed, desperately needed to plant that load of manjuice, my full load of semen, my sperm, my seed, my *cum*, deep up inside Danny. He spread a bit farther open as I neared completion.

With a low growl, in a whispered agony I began to swell inside his tunnel. My cock pulsed once more, then opened in the explosion of my climax. I stroked Dan's dick harder, and as he felt my spasms his own body gave in and he began to buck and moan, growl and then a long strand of thick white cum shot across the back of my hand and onto the sink. We came together, hot and wild, for the second time. I pumped into him, he received it all as he shot his load.

Leaning back into my tight embrace, Danny spurted more. His cum gobbed on my hand as mine pumped and globbed inside his rectum. I felt so complete, so whole in that moment. We stood in a warm, steamy shower room together, my penis deep inside his body, his piss inside my gut. My piss in his belly, my cum up his ass... His cum in my mouth, and our sweat, piss, cum and kisses covered each other. I licked the back of my hand and held him close, then slowly withdrew my softening penis from his asshole.

He turned and looked at me deeply, seeing me licking his spooge. He reached behind himself and then...

Brought up his hand with a full glob of my cum.

He'd let it spurt out into his hand. With deliberate action, slowly and beautifully he raised it to his mouth and began to eat it. His eyes remained locked to mine. A finer toast could never have been. I reached to the sink and took another dollop of his seed and smeared it onto my spunky cock, dripping still with mine. I mixed them. Without a word he leaned down and slurped it off, then rose up to kiss me. We simply stared into each others eyes for a long minute; pleased and whole, completed.

It took a supreme act of will to break away, to gather our clothes and dress. I rolled our piss-wet jocks in a towel and we quietly slipped out of the room. I returned the key to the desk as I had taken it, then we retraced our route back to Danny's truck.

Lying in the bunk together, we turned the radio on low and snuggled. "We'll go for dinner after a bit, OK?"

"Ummm... whatever you say Matt. I'm ready."

I pulled him back onto my chest and we drifted into a deep, contented nap.

Danny and I spent the rest of the afternoon and early evening together in the truck; snuggling, pawing, kissing. Just talking about 'stuff;' enjoying ourselves. He'd had a miserable childhood, youth and school in rural Tennessee. He was actually not too badly adjusted for as fucked-up as his family and young life had been. I felt deeply for him. He honestly had no idea that life could be otherwise than constant pain and turmoil; that most kids' mothers did not tie them into bed or beat them with a broom handle... that most kids' dads did not destroy their homes in drunken rage on a weekly basis. It was painful to listen to him.

I took him to another place for supper, I didn't want to stay at the terminal that much while off the clock. I wasn't too concerned about anyone seeing me or thinking I was fucking him, I truly didn't care. I wasn't ready to go announcing my sexuality, but truth be told I decided regardless of who might see us, I wasn't going to pretend things were otherwise than as they were with Danny.

We had some shitty steaks in a cheap family-type restaurant, then he called in to his dispatcher before returning to the Chattanooga Lines truck. They told him to hang tight, nothing would happen till the middle of the next day anyhow. We stopped on the way and got a 12 pack of beer. I don't think Danny even connected on the significance when we got it, but he wouldn't mind a bit more piss play. I was sure of that. Danny would do whatever I wanted him to; if it pleased me, it would please him to do so. That was nice. And I think he really did connect with the idea of him taking my essence, my manly fluids into his body, the connection of carrying that 'part' of me within himself. The idea turned me on too, always had.

Lying on the bunk again, naked and warm, we popped our 4th beers and I rubbed his belly.

"Hey buddy... these jocks are dry now. Put it on for me OK?"

He smiled and quickly tugged his strap up, onto his body. He laid back, showing himself off in it. He did look fine; tan and smooth, nice muscles and that full bulge. I put mine on also then began the foreplay.

Within a minute we were hot and hard again, slurping and 69'ing, stroking and kissing. We rolled this way and that, turning each other and exploring, licking and sucking one another's bodies from head to toes. We were sweaty and hot in the stuffy truck, but didn't care. The stuffier it became, the more we could smell one another and little else.

I made him acknowledge the action more too; talking and smiling, laughing and enjoying it all. I took his dick from the side of his strap and sucked him, then laughed while his cock was in my mouth. He exploded in laughter, enjoying it insanely.

I rolled Danny onto his belly, then straddled him. I ground the bulge of my jock into his crack, pushing the sweaty, crusty elastic up against his asshole. He squirmed and lifted up, trying to spread his cheeks and offer me his hole. Grinding and humping, I kneaded his cheeks and pulled them apart, then sank down to eat him out again.

He stayed face down, but lifted his pelvis up for me to have better access, to slurp and rim, eat him out and chew on his asshole. I worked him gently, then more forcefully, licking and tonguing, fingering him on and on.

"Yeah man, you like giving me your asshole, don't ya?"

"Mmmmm Matt... man, you can do whatever you want. I just want you to like me."

"Danny, I *liked* you the second I looked at you; I'll always like you."

"I know..." he said softly, smiling, and I was glad he could truly believe it.

I lifted myself up again and once more pressed my hard manhood against him, my jockstrap tight and hot, crusty from the day's play. Pulling the side back once more I let the tip of my cock slide into his crack, just touching his hole. He reached back, his own hands pulling his butt cheeks apart, ready, willing and hoping for what was to come. He needn't have worried...

I took a long deep slug from the can and finished my beer. Looking down, my hairy abdomen was plump, a bit extended, full... "Hey buddy," I whispered in his ear from behind, atop him, "Where's the lube and poppers?"

"Mmmmmmm *grrrrrr*" he grunted, and tried to reach to the side. I picked up the bottle and the white tub and once more slicked my cock, slicked his asshole. He laid his head to the side and closed his eyes, his lips parted. He breathed softly, slowly, calm and waiting for the penetration.

I got into position and began the invasion, my dick hot and hard. The head slipped in and Danny gave a slight "Ummmph!" in horny pleasure. He lifted up a bit and straightened his tube. My cock slid effortlessly into him the full length. I was in him once more, and began a slow, full stroke, fucking into his butt.

I moved my legs a bit, then laid atop him, full length, Danny impaled beneath me. Licking the back of his neck and around to his face, I then was able to kiss him while fucking him from behind. He slurped, sucked on my tongue. I cracked the bottle of amyl and offered him the first snort. He lifted his head, I held it for him on both sides, one... two... three deep hits. Then I hit deeply and slow.

I relaxed and lay my hairy chest on his smooth back, then whispered in his ear.

"Dan... Danny..."

"Mmmmmm...?"

"I'm filling you man, I'm pumping you full..." As my slit flared within his rectum, the tube of my cock swelled and filled, and I began to piss. I flexed the muscles of my bladder and cock, and he groaned aloud.

"*Ugggh*... oh?" He pushed back to me, trying to force me in deeper.

"I'm *pissing* in you man... *pissing*..."

"Oooooh... ahhh... Oh GOD MATT! I can feel it! Oh yes! I can *FEEL* it! Give it to me, fill me up! Oh god man! *Yeahhhhhhhhhhhh!*"

"Yeah buddy, that's it... open up to me, take it Danny, take my piss man... that's it." I crooned in his ear as I pissed into him. I pressed a bit harder, deeper, and felt the head of my cock slip against the second ring, and open his colon. I relaxed, hit the poppers again and FORCED myself to piss, piss hard and full, not regulating my flow. "Yeah buddy, all that piss for you, just for you man... take it... ummmmmmm"

"Oh Matt... Matt! Fuck! Matt! OH GOD MAN YEAHHH!" He clenched his eyes, then tried to turn to look into my face. I moved across him and looked deeply at him from behind. The golden eyes flashed wildly, then filled with moisture. One droplet ran down his cheek, then another. He sobbed, moaned and began to cry... in sheer joy.

"Oh god Matt! Fuck me man, piss in me! Oh god do it! Yes! Oh man, YES!" My bladder was still under pressure, plenty remained, and I forced one more hard hot stream into him, deep, *deep* into his intestine, then slowed and began to pull back and forth, fucking his ass while I poured manly piss into him. The fullness was too much and a nice burst was forced back, splashing out onto his butt, onto my jock and down his balls, onto the padding on the bunk. We could hear it.

"Oh fuck man! *Oh GOD!.*" Tears ran down his face.

I paused the stream, knowing I'd given him about half my bladderful; and drinking beer I could hold over a liter. There was already a pint, 3 cups of hot piss inside him.

And plenty more to feed him...

I pulled back slowly, he looked confused, again the thought that he was being spurned, rejected, was obvious in his expression. But I quickly leaned down and kissed him, his tears still hot and wet on his face.

"Don't worry buddy, I'm giving you more man... more... I want you to feel this..." and slid my cock under his scrotum from behind, the head of my hot meat slipping into his jock pouch. He smiled, closed his eyes and waited, submitted. I paused again and offered him poppers. He took a snort and so did I, then once more...

I began to piss. Right up into his jock, right into the sheet and under him a hot stream started to flow, wetting and marking his genitals. Then I pulled back, out and moved him onto his back. Getting up onto my knees, I offered him my wet dripping cock, offering to feed him. He accepted instantly, lifting up on his hands and leaning forward as my cock jumped. Quickly he had me in position, his lips wrapped around me just behind the corona.

I huffed poppers once more, then...

Opened. Piss flowed for him.

Piss. He moaned as he nursed, taking gulp after sweet gulp of my fine beer piss. He drank and swallowed, I pissed slowly and perfectly. He didn't lose a drop.

The last of my stream tapered down, then one more nice spurt. I was empty, drained and Danny was grinning like a madman.

"Man... fuck Matt. God this is hot..." I smiled back, then kissed him again. His kisses were like silk, every one a treat. I reached into the pouch of his jock, then began to jack him. Grease from lubing his hole and my cock was still on my hand and it was enough to bring him off in about 40 seconds. He lay back and bucked, moaning softly as he clenched his eyes closed and swooned in his orgasm. His cum spurted up, across my hand, onto his body.

I licked a large gob from my hand and kissed him. I smeared the remainder fully onto the front of his jock, then lay alongside him to blow my load. I cradled him and kissed as I stroked myself, Danny looking down between kisses to watch in fascination. Then I began to buck and groan, my balls hot and boiling.

I grunted, "Oh man, here it cums... Danny here it *Cums* buddy!" and in a second he was down before me, mouth open. I flopped my cock free from my hand and he slurped it, sucked it into his mouth right to the bush in a flash. My first spurt was hot, hard and tight, but only a daub of cum came out. The next spurt, and those following though, were hot, full and violent. I spurted 4 or 5 full hot gobs into his gullet, then a few more dribbles. He gulped, sucked and took it all with his eyes closed in joy.

I finished and collapsed alongside him, my cock still throbbing and jumping. A strand of cum was strung from my slit to his mouth, to his chin, linking us. I broke free and kissed him in the spooge, what he hadn't already swallowed. I laid him back.

For long moments we said nothing, just caressed and floated on the bunk. Finally the wetness of the bed got to us and we rose, quietly cleaning up and putting a fresh sheet on the mat. We made ready at last to sleep, to go to bed in the literal sense. Danny had toweled off a bit, and seemed as if he would remove his jockstrap. I stopped him.

"Sleep in it with me, OK? With me... do it *For* me...?"

He smiled again, ready. "Oh yes sir! Whuttevuh you like! He leaned back, pulled me beside him close, my own jock still damp and spunky also. I put my arm across him and made him secure. I pulled his man-scented wool blanket up over us and nestled in.

In 10 minutes, less, we were fast asleep. The rhythm of Danny's peaceful breathing lulled me to sleep. I don't think my cock ever did soften completely that night...

TUCSON

We awoke well before dawn, the darkness still profound. A gleam from the terminal's parking lot lights filtered in the side window. I rustled and Danny lifted his head from the cradle of my arm.

"Ummmm" he groaned and stretched. "You're still here..."

I smiled. "Yeah buddy, I am. I told you I wanted to stay the night. I wanted to wake up next to you, man."

He smiled broadly. Despite our mung-y morning mouths, we swapped a quick kiss, then began to get ourselves up. I lifted myself up and watched him awakening. He stretched, smiled and grunted.

Swinging my legs over the edge of the bunk I stretched, groaning loudly. I gathered up my clothes slowly and began to dress. I reached over and ran my hand up Dan's body, down his belly and across the bulge in his jock pouch. His cock was still thick, the strap still a bit moist and funky, coated with several layers of piss and cum.

"I didn't know if you would be here or not. I'm glad you stayed."

"Wouldn't have missed it Dan." I slipped into my pants, then T-shirt. Danny started to haul himself out of the bunk and I handed him his pile of clothing.

"I'm going to have to call dispatch by 7:00," he began. "I need to figure out the route and all, see when I'm leaving..."

I paused a moment and thought about it. "Are you coming back this way after you make that drop?"

"I don't know, depends on them. Don't know what route I'll take..."

I pawed him once again. "Make sure you do. Tell them you have a need and <u>have</u> to come back. Maybe I'll do it myself..."

He smiled, really pleased. "You want to see me again?"

"Sure do man. You gotta come back."

He grunted assent, then tried to get up from the bunk. "Man I've got to get to the john!" I realized we had not left the vehicle since returning from dinner.

"You didn't get up during the night?"

"No." *He still had that full load of my piss up his ass too.* Wow.

Without thinking about it, I flipped my zipper open and offered him my cock. "Here, a sip before you go out." He grinned, and leaned forward. We'd had enough beer the night before. It would be thicker than what he'd had, but wasn't full-strength 'morning piss' either. I shot a nice slow stream for him as he gulped, then pulled back and spurted a small dose onto his belly and jock. "There."

I handed him his pants and boots. "Here." Quickly he got into them and grabbed his shirt, then carefully got to the door. "I'll be right back..." I nodded; I'd finished my own preparations before he got back. I decided I'd buy a shirt at the supply shop; the rest of my gear was fine.

Upon returning, he climbed back in and once more I embraced him, kissing slowly. He pulled some fresh clothes from the bin and once more undressed. He began to pull his jockstrap down and I stopped him.

"Danny?" He looked at me expectantly. "I want you to keep that on till you come back to me. Keep that on until _I_ take it off you, OK?"

He smiled widely. "OK... you mean wear it the whole time? Just take it off to shower, that kind of thing?"

"No man, I mean you don't take it off, *period*. You're not permitted to shower. Wash yourself with a cloth. Keep it on while you piss. Pull it aside and piss around it, piss through it, but you wear it. You don't take it off to shit; pull it up and away, but you wear it. It's OK if you find someone who wants to fuck, you're allowed to have sex, but you wear it while he does." I paused.

"If he gives you piss, make him put some on it, and you wear it. If he cums in your mouth, smear some on the jock, if he cums up your ass, dip some out and smear it on there and you wear it."

He was grinning brightly, really fascinated and pleased. I was giving him his orders.

"Jack off if you need to, but shoot your load into it and you wear it." I dropped my voice, low and fine, seductive. A whisper: "You have our piss and sweat, our cum and slobber on you now man. You got *me* on there with you... don't take me off OK? Take me with you, *keep* me with you..." Once more I thought he would cry for joy.

"Yes! Oh YES! Yes Sir, I will!" He knew it would be a mission, a test of endurance, a marathon. I knew he'd still be in it, have it fused to his skin when he got back.

The first rays of morning were beginning to filter through the windows; we got ourselves ready for parting, though neither of us wanted to. Making small talk again, this and that... how the road would be, how long it would take. Who the company might send him to replace George; and I assured him I would find out immediately about his former teammate. Then I asked him about his trip back to the building.

"How was it when you went to the toilet?"

He looked down, embarrassed, but wanting me to know. "Um, well... uhhh... it was gross. I mean, well... but... but I liked it! I can't tell you..."

I chuckled a bit. "I bet! But it was hot though, wasn't it? I know I gave you a lot... Could you smell it?"

Once more he grinned in perversion. "Man! Yes I could! It wasn't like usual piss, but... it was *rank*, bitter, like a urinal. *I* was a _urinal_. I never done any of that before Matt. You done that to me... damn man... but... I like it! I really do..." He added in a whisper, "With _you_ I like it..."

I touched him on the shoulder. "You didn't pull your jock down while you sat did you?"

He almost blushed, again his body telling me of his embarrassment, but also his pleasure at our perverted scene. "No, no man. I didn't! I wanted to keep it on!"

"Good boy. Damn I'm proud of you. And I know you'll do what I told you to too..." I kissed him, then moved to the door.

"I have to get myself ready for the office, man. Stop by in an hour." He nodded. I shifted tone, shifted gears, shifted roles.

"Alright Chattanooga, you come by the office and let me know when this cluster-fuck is gonn' be off the tarmac here. If you cain't get a forklifter by 10:00, I'll talk to C.L. dispatch m'seff."

He nodded, trying to get back to trucking himself. His cowboy swagger, his bravado came back in a flash, but it wasn't complete. "Yeah OK Sir, um, Matt. Will do. Gonn' call them by 7:00 anyhow." The submission he'd found with me remained.

"Good. Talk to you in a bit." With that, I hopped down from the step onto the pavement, and snapped the door shut, leaving Danny behind the glass. I knew he would watch me go around the corner of the building, but I didn't want him to know I saw his tears.

I took my time. I went out to my car, on the far side of the employee lot and got a clean T-shirt. Then I headed into the supply shop and bought a light blue work shirt. The clerk eyed me; I don't know what she thought, but I didn't really care either. Another greasy twat with an IQ of about 72... 'Room temperature intelligence,' Bill Barlow had called it. I chuckled, then went into the men's room to change.

The second I opened the door and whiffed the air, my bladder just about exploded. I hadn't pissed since beer drinking and fucking either... I stepped to urinal and fumbled to open my fly. My sticky jockstrap hampered me a bit, and I was already dripping and flowing by the time I got my dick pointed into the porcelain. I licked the drops from my fingers while pissing and splashing. It took a long 2 minutes.

I stripped off my shirts and changed into the clean ones. I tucked in, straightening my jock and enjoying the funky dampness. Then I headed back out into the hallway, past the shop. I bought a large paper cup of coffee on my way to the control booth. Doug was finishing his clean up and I tossed my dirty shirts onto the chair as came in. He grinned, smacked me on the shoulder.

"Hey man, morning. Take it you didn't bother to go home last night?" His question was genuine, but he had no idea where it was leading. "I saw your car was still here when I came in last night; hasn't moved since then either." He waited for an answer. I said nothing. "You find something nice last night?"

I grinned and still said nothing, flexing my eyebrows in an expression of, "Don't you wish you knew?!?!?"

He shoved the night's log sheets onto the counter, then sat on the wooden chair. "Did you hear anything about that trucker you sent outta here Doc?" I told him I was going to check with Dr. MacKenzie by 9:00 when we saw Danny come around from the side of the shop. He walked as he had when I first saw him, his loneliness so obvious to me now. Doug watched him without comprehending.

Dan approached, then stuck his head in the door just like the previous morning. "I talked to my dispatch there Matt." He looked confused. "I don't know what I'm supposed to do. There's no other driver and no forkers within a couple hundred miles of here. Team finishing a drop in Gary, Indiana... They said maybe get some men here around 7:00 tonight." I snorted.

"OK man... _I'll_ deal with it." Doug was curious, but went to punch out. I was on the phone with a Chattanooga dispatch supervisor when he got back.

"Yeah that's what I said, girl. Now you TELL your manager that's how it's going to be. This is not a _question_. I've got 118 scheduled trucks on this lot right now; and I'm not leaving this load of fuckin' timber out there tippin' sideways on one of your goddam trailers. NOW YOU LISTEN TO _ME_..." I paused. The surprise on Doug's face was funny, amazing.

"I have a qualified forker right here; we are going to restack that trailer and your driver is going to be taking the davit with him. He's going to leave this afternoon and head to Tucson alone; we are NOT waiting for your pencil-dicks to show up god-only-knows when. He's going to make the drop at Chamberlain and Davis-Monthan and you are going to have the terminal expecting this load. When he does, he's going to pick up the very next load scheduled for Minneapolis-Hennepin and he's going to RETURN to this facility with our equipment. You are going to be billed for the forklift operator at YOUR pay rate; and you are going to reimburse us without complaints. *Do you understand?*" There were a few more comments, but they quickly acquiesced.

Dan was smiling wonderfully, but didn't speak until I'd slammed the phone down. "I guess I gotta come back here then huh?" The *oh-poor-ME* tone was obvious. *Don't throw me in the briar patch!*

I grinned back and smacked him upside the shoulder, hard. "Yeah cowboy, you <u>do</u>. Now go get some grub. Tell Tina in the coffee shop it's voucher #6, got it? Number <u>six</u>. We'll make your supers pay for that too. Hehehe. OK, I'm gonna get the rest of this shit done." Danny nodded and walked out. He turned and paused, looked back at us just before rounding the corner to the coffee shop. Doug watched that fine man walking away in fascination, his understanding dawning.

"Hmmm. I think I *know* where you spent the night, Matt!" he chuckled. I looked at him hard. "Hey, don't get me wrong buddy! You never know, I might take a poke at something like <u>that</u> myself!"

My smile turned real ugly real fast. I didn't mean to snarl or challenge Doug by any means, but it came out clear and wild, protective, possessive and intensely sexual. I spoke slowly, clearly, each word a morsel of venom.

"*The fucking hell you will.* You keep your goddam hands <u>off</u> that boy; he got a world of trouble you don't know <u>nothing</u> about, and you are NOT going to add to it."

It was his turn to shift gears without the clutch. "Man! Hey... HEY!" He backed up a step. "I didn't mean anything by it! Hey, it's ok! You got something going, I ain't gonna get in the way man! I just didn't know you were..." I glanced at him sharply. "Um, ah... nothing man. I ain't gonna say nothing. Ever."

That wasn't why I relaxed, but with an effort I pulled my emotions under control and was able to speak in a normal tone.

"I really don't give a shit if you do or don't. I DO give a shit about HIM. You leave him alone and you make damn sure everyone else does too." I took a slow breath. "And I don't just mean about sex..."

Doug breathed slowly and deeply too. He smiled in a genuine, respectful way. "You got it Doc!" He made ready to leave and chuckled. "Goddam buddy, if I'm ever in trouble... I hope to fuck you're on _my_ side." He punched me on the upper arm and headed to the door. Now it was my turn to laugh.

"Doug... I am man. I am."

For the next week things went smoothly at Hennepin. Greg was on time, Doug was thorough. Mike Wales had called our seasonal staff meeting. We gathered in the coffee shop one morning at 9:00. All the 'managers' were present.

Mike gave me a company commendation for 'saving the life' of a worker. George'd done ok under Dr. MacKenzie's care, but had gone back to Montgomery to retire. (And the good doctor had told me how funny it was at the hospital. They put George in a private room, but nurses, orderlies and other doctors alike were in hysterics about Lil Mac K treating him, checking on ovaries and vaginal warts and hysterectomies, then going in to see the groady, blubbery trucker from Alabama...)

Mike had also sent a memo around about the lot-runners getting out of hand again and how all personnel should report any 'suspicious' behavior at the facility. Doug lost his mind when he heard that one.

"Holy shit! Doesn't he know the pain and suffering he'll cause, taking away INCOME from all those women? Er, girls? Er... uh... um, yeah,

THEM?" We laughed uproariously. Mike didn't think we were funny, which made it all the funnier. "What's Ming Li going to do to feed those babies?" Doug asked, and there was another round of hysteria.

"She changed her name," I volunteered, having had a most memorable conversation with my father. I'd told him about the Vietnamese call-boy. He told me about his days in 'Nam; he'd been there in the late 50's, before the US was in combat.

"The one we knew in Da Nang," he'd said, "We called *Sum Yung Phuc*." I explained this for everyone. Mike and Greg howled; even Tina, and Cindy the dumb babe from the supply shop thought it was funny. Doug laughed along with us, but asked me to explain it when the others had gone. I wrote it out for him and he laughed all the more.

"Man! You don't know how much you help me Matt. This shit with *letters* you know... I just can't get it. Never could."

"We make an OK team here Doug. No problem." We finished our coffee and got up from the table. Doug took his time and I knew there was more. Both of us were off that day, there being now 3 new part-timers on the team.

"You wanna go get a beer?" he asked. It was well past 11:00, so I agreed. He drove us to a pub just up the highway from the terminal and we got a table. The doors were open, the warmth of June now beautiful. He took a long time to get to the point, staring into his beer and fiddling with a pack of cigarettes. As far as I'd known, he didn't even smoke.

But he finally got to the subject at hand. "Matt, I talked to Joe Dothan down at the terminal in Tucson. Dan Meinrad was there a few days ago. Seems he got into some trouble."

I sucked my breath in a little too quickly, but waited.

"He's OK man, he's ok. Got smacked around I guess, nothing too serious. But..." He looked down, then directly at me.

"Chattanooga fired him. His super heard about it and that was that. They wired him his trip pay and took the rig. He's done."

"Man..." I said. "How the hell...?" Doug stopped me.

"Some fucker from Texas, invited him to his rig for beer. Guess Danny thought he wanted 'more' than company for TV and a brew, and they got into it." Doug was upset, he was taking it almost as seriously as he knew I would.

"What the hell's he going to do? You know anything?"

Doug smiled and continued. "Yeah man, I do. I got some buddies in 'Zona and Texas too. We got a few bucks together. Got him a plane ticket." I looked at him, waiting. "I told those guys about you man..." He paused. I didn't react.

"Danny's gotta get home to Tennessee you know. But we thought maybe he should come here for a few days first. He'll be in late tonight. I thought maybe you'd wanna take him to your place...?"

I was my turn to wonder. "Doug... I don't know what to say. I mean... yes. I do. I want that a lot." I looked down into my beer a long time. Danny beaten; fired and rejected again. Suddenly I felt as though I had been hit in the guts; I wanted to puke, literally. But Doug and guys I didn't even know had taken it upon themselves to help him. To help us...

"Doug..." I paused as he looked at me.

"Thank you."

"Naw man, it's nothing. Ain't a meatball..." I smiled weakly at his 'shop talk.'

The waitress came by and asked if we needed another round. I started to say 'no,' but Doug ordered for us both. "There's more I wanna talk about," he said.

He paid the ugly broad when our beers came and then got to it, no nonsense. "Matt, I've met someone. Someone special. Someone *real* special."

I nodded. "Oh yeah? Good for you man..."

"Someone like Danny..."

Wow.

"Doug... that's great. I'm real happy. But what... what can I do for ya?"

"I just need to talk man. It's so weird, so different. I never met anyone..." he paused and looked down a long time. "I never met *anyone* like Dave. I got divorced 4 years ago, been alone ever since. Is that why I like him?" He looked up, his eyes were different. He wasn't going to tear up, but there was an intensity, the pain of it we're all so familiar with.

"Is it just cause I'm lonely? How can I suddenly want to be with... with him? With a *guy*?" He sipped his beer and finally lit up a smoke. He exhaled slowly as I sought my words. "You know about it Matt... you're into it. I saw how Danny looked at you, how you looked at him. At *me*... How you'd just kill anyone who'd hurt him."

I let him continue.

"That's just how I feel about Dave. It makes me feel... he makes me feel like I'm the only other man in the whole world; like I'd fuckin' kill anyone who would ever do anything to him... Am I a fag?"

I had to laugh at that, and it was not the right time to laugh. He was deeply insulted, hurt. I had to smooth it over right quick.

"Doug, no. Well, I don't know. Am I? I don't know that either. Lemme tell you how I feel about it, and maybe it'll make some sense. First off, you don't 'suddenly' want to be with him; you needed him for a long time. I dunno what any of us do." The plural, 'us,' including him, already made him feel better. He wasn't alone.

"I got a lot to give someone, someone special. I don't know what all that means, what all it's gotta be, but I know it when I'm with that person. Now Danny..." Doug listened intently, he really wanted to hear about this.

"Danny came up to us and I knew, just *knew* we needed to know each other. Really know it all... To talk, laugh... Cry. I needed to explore him, see how he ticks. And yes, his body is hot, he's fine. I wanted to get naked and nasty, get close and personal. I wanted to taste him and touch him and hold him... I wanted to *fuck*..." Doug was nodding fast, his eyes sparkling.

"YES! I met Dave and he looked at me, and when I looked at him I saw *into* him. And I just wanted more. More... I don't even know what. But... he done... we done things I never thought I'd ever do."

"Yeah, I know. But Doug... does he make you feel good?"

"Oh man... oh yes. Yes."

"Well then, only you can say if *that* makes you a fag or homo or whatever. But if you got something with Dave you can't find anywhere else, then goddam it, take it! Remember about Danny? You said you wouldn't say anything, wouldn't put us in jeopardy. You meant around work and all..." He nodded; he remembered it word for word I was sure.

"Well it's the same thing here man. I ain't gonna say anything but the important part is this. You got a guy, someone who cares about you, wants and needs you. Loves you? Maybe so... and you him." I paused and took a drink from my mug. "You can open up to him like nobody else, not ever before and prolly not later. Just you and him, and that's all that matters. You and Dave."

"Here's what I think about it. Tonight it's gonna be me and Danny. At my house, in my bed. Now nobody and I damn well mean <u>nobody</u> is gonna tell me who can come to bed with me and who can't. There's nobody in the world whose business that is but Danny and me."

"I always liked men, liked lookin' at guys, you know? Their bodies, their dicks... in school, the gym you know? Maybe you did too?" He was nodding, smiling. "I'm not going to run around with hearts and flowers, I'm not going to start wearing silk blouses and high heels, but for now, that's my guy. My man. That's all there is to it. And it's between me and him, not *anyone* else."

Doug was already taking the next step. He might've been dyslexic, but he was damn smart. "Yeah man, I get it. And nobody gotta know; Dave don't come in but once-twice a month." Suddenly I knew who Dave was, a driver from Utah. In his mid-40's, nice looking, well built and soft spoken, and from what I could surmise a good hot topman. Doug had done real well there.

"Nobody's gotta know Doug. And they won't ever hear nothing from me."

He smiled, sighed and finished his beer. "Yeah, I know Matt. I trust you. But I trust Dave too. I gotta have more of him man. I need him. I want... I want to be with him."

"Then let's get the hell out of here and go find our boys!" He laughed aloud and we got up from the table.

"Yeah! Let's go get 'em!" We made small talk on the way back to his car.

"How did you know he was right?" Doug asked.

"Well, that butt for one thing... and his keys on the right." Doug needed to hear about the codes... "Then there was the *jockstrap*... hehehe."

"How'd'you know he was wearing a jockstrap?"

"The lines on his butt. And that just made me want to fuck that beautiful ass all the more! I always wear one too..." There was more, chatting and laughing as Doug became a bit more secure, a bit more comfortable being gay. He wanted to hear all about it: what we'd done, how it felt, why I liked what I liked. I told him much, but by <u>no</u> means everything. He wanted to go with me to the airport to get Danny, but had to see if Dave wanted to join us too.

He couldn't wait to have Dave's cock up his ass again, you could tell.

BRANDED

I'd gone home to get some things ready for my guest, and Doug went his way. He said he'd call and the phone rang at 9:20. I had been pacing for hours, unable to nap, unable to do much of anything but watch the second hand tick around the clock again and again. I picked it up quickly, "Hello?"

"Hey man, you ready to head up to the airport?"

"Like I can think of anything else?"

He laughed. "I got the map to your house. I hope you don't mind but... is it OK if Dave comes with us?"

"Damn right man, you know it," I said. "I'm ready."

Doug wanted to pick me up, all drive together, but I mentioned we might need to part company, depending on the shape Danny was in. He understood, and I grabbed my keys, agreeing to meet him at the Northwest Orient (*"Bwannnnnnnnnggg!"*) Aaaaiir-liiiiiines main ticket counter. We'd find the concourse and gate from there.

As it happened, we pulled into the new parking structure at almost exactly the same second. I led the way to the 3rd level and we parked in a rearward corner. The level was all but deserted. We got out of our cars and Dave walked up to me first, hand outstretched.

"Hey Matt; great to meet you in person!" he said. "Actually we have, but that's a bit different huh?" I had to agree. Doug was a bit unsure of himself. He was torn between a kind of paranoia and utmost pride, going out in public with his new *boyfriend*. The inward tension was resulting in a form of borderline panic, I thought.

We shrugged it off with a bit of 'shop' talk, laughing about the staff meeting and Sum Yung Phuc. It took less than a minute and Doug was as calm and secure beside Dave and me as he could ever have been. We got to the ticket counter and found we had less than 15 minutes 'til the flight from Phoenix arrived. Doug said that Joe Dothan had driven Danny up to Phoenix himself, rather than making him stay in Tucson or take the other flights. We hustled up to the correct gate as they were announcing the arrival as 10:44. Deboarding would be in 5 minutes.

The roar of jets became louder and louder, and the distinctive form of a Boeing 727 appeared in the window with its 'T' tail and 3rd engine. We stood shoulder to shoulder, away from the passenger gathering area of carpet and horrible couches, staying on the tiled walkway and watching for the jetway door to open. The digital clock flipped its page to 10:43 and the doorway opened, a maroon-clad stewardess emerging first. In a matter of seconds the stream of passengers began to stalk through the door and into the lounge. Families were reunited, lovers embraced, businessmen and students toting their bags of crap walked away alone. It went on and on... 40... 60... 100 people. The stream of bodies thinned, became sporadic. Another... then one more.

I craned my neck to see into the jetway. The captain and copilot emerged, then 2 more stewardesses. Then, at last, a tall man in a blue baseball cap and snug faded Levi's. He slouched a bit, his shoulders almost rounded. He didn't look up as he shuffled, his dusty boots telling of a long road of pain. I stepped forward to meet him, and had to stop him in mid-stride.

"Danny?" He looked up, almost shocked to see me. I waited for a reaction.

"Matt," he said softly. "Matt... oh god..." Once more I thought he would burst into tears. His face was bruised, a distinct black-and-blue smudge beneath his left eye, his cheek reddened and scraped. His upper lip was noticeably swollen on the left as well. Fuck.

We paused for a long second as I slowly lifted my hand to touch him, making contact on his upper chest. Doug and Dave came up behind me; Doug was trying to say hello, 'hey howdy' or some such, but we didn't hear him. I looked at Danny, sharing his pain. I ached from heart to heels looking at him. Without a word I slowly wrapped my arms around him and pulled him in close. He grunted low and soft as I enveloped him in my body, then...

I lifted his chin to face me directly and pulled him in close to kiss him.

For long, long moments I held him, our mouths united and our breathing as one. I licked his tongue, held him by his ass cheeks, my arms tight around him. Silently we kissed, then backed apart only a bit, still holding our arms around each other. A few tears coursed down both our faces. I kissed one from his bruised cheek.

Doug was beside me, standing quietly as I finally backed away from the fine cowboy. "Nobody's ever, _ever_ gonn' do that to you again man," I said. Doug nodded and spoke.

"Hey Danny, glad you made it..." Dave grunted similar thoughts, soft and reassuring. Danny brightened quickly, the change remarkable in its velocity and completeness. It was a change he'd made before, from the tears of one or another horrendous beating back to himself.

"Man I know... it's OK. I know... You're here. I came back Matt, just like you told me to." I grabbed his hand and pulled him away from the gate area. I was finally able to notice the people in the concourse. There were more than a few staring in various shades of shock and disbelief.

It was 1978 and men kissing in <u>that</u> kind of a way in public was all but un-fucking-heard of. I heard one man mumble 'fuckin' faggots' and his girlfriend or wife shushing him. We ignored them all.

We walked quickly down to baggage, then out to the parking structure. Dave and Doug were quiet, intimate, as were Danny and me. I wrapped an arm around Dan's waist, held his hand even. They weren't ready for that kind of display; Danny really wasn't either, so I knocked it off. I'd made my point at the gate upstairs.

But at the cars, behind the concrete pylons shielding all of us from view even if there had been someone else up there, I once more pulled him against my body and kissed him slowly, passionately. He closed his eyes and held me; I groped his butt cheeks as we made out.

"Dan, what are you wearing?"

He pushed back a bit and grinned. "Man... you know what I got on under here. You tole' me..."

I smiled smugly as Dave and Doug stared quizzically. I patted his ass again. "Tell 'em, buddy."

He looked almost sheepish, but complied. "I got my jockstrap on..."

You could see the horny gleam in Doug's eye. "You mean the *same*... the one you spotted first?" Danny nodded and I spoke.

"Yup. The same one. I tole' him to keep it on. I fucked him in it... he's _fine_ lookin' in a jockstrap, man."

Dave chuckled too. "I damn bet he is!" and we all laughed. Danny was only slightly self-conscious, he heartily needed and accepted the admiration.

"I still got mine on too, Dan."

Now he was really pleased; I'd shared the experience with him! He smiled low, then leaned in to kiss me. I was sure that he himself had never initiated such a thing in his life, that 'public' kiss. He murmured in my ear. "Let's go home... take me home, Matt."

We broke off our embrace and quickly made our parting from the others. I had Danny on the passenger seat not 40 seconds later and just as quickly was in the car myself, slapping it into gear and pulling away. The warm night surrounded us as we backed out. But as we lurched forward, we could just glimpse Dave in the shadows, pressing Doug up against the concrete wall, making out in the parking lot!

I got us home quickly and we headed straight to the bedroom. While I wanted to take our time, enjoy Danny and our foreplay, we were way too hot, too needing. I yanked his shirt back, kissing him and sucking, chewing his nipples. Then our boots and jeans, down to our spunky, scented jockstraps.

Dan's was pasted to his body, stuck into his flesh as I'd expected it would be. Mine wasn't much different. The outlines of our straps were reddish, nubby and distinct. It looked almost like we'd been jockstrap-branded. The waistband of his white Bike showed two distinct, thick lines of blood. Indeed, he'd *not* taken it off...

"Man, what the...?"

He looked down at himself, then explained. "I met this guy, big hairy fucker; a 'Will' something. He asked if I wanted to meet up and we did. He fucked me and then he wanted me to take it off. I wouldn't. He got mad, said you weren't there and had no business controlling our sex... he punched me."

"Wow."

"I punched him back and busted his face too and got the hell out. Next day though, he'd told some guys that I had tried to get fresh with him and he fought me off. Had to make up something about getting his face blacked up I guess. I tried to ell 'em it was him too, but they didn't listen. *I* got fired. Fuck 'em."

He was a bit agitated telling me the events. I calmed him with stroking and kissing, then got him on the bed. His legs up and apart, I dove in to eat him out while my own cock jumped and oozed. He'd washed and kept himself fairly clean, but he was ripe, funky and hot. Manly.

I greased us up quickly and yanked my strap aside. I shoved my cock into his hot hole with fury, and it was like the very first time we'd fucked. I simply buried my cock in him to the hilt and did not stroke at all; in seconds we had both bucked and shot our loads. We simply laid back and snuggled. There would be more, later.

At 2:35 AM the phone rang again. It was Doug; Danny lifted his head from the pillow and smiled, coming up from a light sleep nestled in my armpit.

"We're still up, I figured you guys would be too," Doug said. "I wanted to see how things... I mean, what you were doing... um, ah..."

"Hehehe, yeah. It's OK, Doug. We were snoozing a bit; we fucked as soon as we got home. How you guys doing?" I knew dang well Dave was still with him. Dave was relieved I was congenial, it was kind of a personal thing to be asking about at such a weird hour, but I didn't care. I knew Dan wouldn't either. I paused a moment. Doug said nothing, waiting, so I continued.

"We kept our jockstraps on..." Doug sucked his breath in quickly; that was exactly what he wanted to know about. "But, we been in those things for 2 weeks, we FINALLY took 'em off!" I could hear Dave rustling in the background, probably with his ear up to the side of the phone too.

"We got 'em on the floor, we showered and now we're naked and snuggled up. The marks though... we're both branded with jockstrap marks."

"Wow! Dang man, that's hot..." I knew he wanted to tell _me_ more; tell me about Dave and him. He was new, amazed by everything, and needed to express the joy, the pure sexuality, the pure _freedom_ of it all. I was sure he and Dave had talked; but he needed to talk to me, to someone who was not a sex partner but who could understand it too.

"Yeah we just got cleaned up too. Dave turned me a different way tonight. I was on my back... I could kiss him while we were... while..."

"Go ahead Doug, say it!"

"While he _fucked_ me!"

The pure horny elation of admitting he had been _fucked_, and how much he liked it was a catharsis for him. Cleansing, purifying, liberating. I had no information about his marriage, how happy or unhappy he'd been. But it was obvious he'd been needing a hot, hard cock in his mouth and ass for a long, _long_ time. Finally he had one... it was beautiful.

"Let me say _Hey_ to Dave." He was glad to put his man on the phone.

"Hehehe, settin' the boy free huh?" Dave laughed a bit too, and smirked.

"Well I'm not sure how good a guide I am to set someone 'free.' I live in Salt Lake City you know..."

"Dave, you got him naked and enjoying his own body, enjoying yours. That's more freedom than that boy has had all his life. Make him love it man, be good to him, OK?"

Dave agreed, and put Doug back on. "Matt... we're gonna go back to bed now man. You take care, see you day after tomorrow huh?" Danny had been listening with a peaceful smile on his face. He wanted to get back to privacy too.

I hung up the phone and nestled in close to Dan. "Mmmmmmm buddy... I'm so glad you're here, you're in one piece."

"Me too, Matt. Thanks... *thank you* for getting me back, man," he whispered.

I kissed him and we drifted into a deep, peaceful sleep.

The few days with Danny went quickly; we knew we were on borrowed time, that it would be coming to an end. But we made the most of the chance we did have. Upon waking from our reunion night, I kept him in his jockstrap the whole of the following day, jumping on him, fucking, sucking and playing whenever I felt like it. He enjoyed himself thoroughly, but his main concern was what he was going to do for a job since the circumstances of being fired from Chattanooga Lines weren't exactly a good reference.

"Man I'll get by, I know I'll find something. Hell, I was lookin' for a job when I found that one, you know?" I thought that was a good way to look at it.

The guys had figured on three nights; and Dan's tickets back to Tennessee weren't refundable. I don't think we would've changed the arrangement anyhow. But too soon it was time for him to go home. The night before, Dave and Doug took us to a nice dinner, talking and laughing. The merriment hid an unspoken tension, Danny's fears and trepidation at what he'd find upon returning to his family home. They had been unaware of his proclivities, but a shitty stunt from Chattanooga made sure an unexpected and unnecessary call to his home tipped them off.

"I don't know what Dad and Marla will do," he said, meaning his dad's young wife. "They's pretty tied up in that church and all, holy rollin'. It's a big sin you know..." Oh I knew; heard it all my life. "I'll have to find myself a small place right quick, maybe get out of Bradley County. My brothers went on down to Valdosta, Donny drives for Schneider and Dicky's a plant foreman." He sighed.

"Donny's cool with me; Dicky ain't gonn' wanna see me none though." I pulled him onto my shoulder, leaning back against the big headboard as we watched TV, not hearing or seeing it. That was the only light on in the room.

"We're gonna get you set up Danny; don't worry about it now. It'll all work out." He smiled, wanting to believe me. Truthfully I had no idea what, if anything, I might be able to do for him. I kissed him gently and stroked his body. He leaned back and let me take over. Quickly I had him undressed; but again in the same jockstrap he'd been wearing for almost 3 weeks.

As had become almost routine with us, kissing and exploring his body lead to him on his back, legs up for me to suck and lick, eat him out. Then getting into a hot 69, humping into his face as I fingered and probed, tongued his asshole, I prepared him for fucking. He writhed slowly, gently, and had become very adept at clenching and opening his ass for me. Before going to dinner with the other guys, we'd fucked for over a solid hour, but neither of us had cum. Consciously we'd decided to save it till now.

He had gotten better at expressing himself while having sex, yet still was not one to talk much. When he did his voice was soft, secretive. Even between him and me alone, locked in our refuge, he was reticent. I wasn't sure if it perhaps was a kind of guilt, not totally acknowledging his nature even to himself. Maybe it was just his own way of focusing, of keeping the action private, lest the walls and furniture invade the intimacy of our sexual coupling.

I slid my tongue down the inside of his thigh, and took his already rock-hard cock into my warm mouth. He raised his hips, stroking my head while I worked him. His precum oozed and ran, we were both almost as desperate to shoot our loads as that very first time we'd had sex. I lifted his legs, raised his pelvis to rim and tongue him. He moaned and ground onto me, ready. Very quietly, softly he asked...

"Mmmmm, *fuck* me please... Fuck me now, Sir?" Drawing his legs over my shoulders and getting into position, I leaned down to kiss him slowly as I penetrated, entered him in a greasy, wonderful slide. We groaned together, then he began a much harder, forceful bucking, wanting me to hump and rape his hole. I pressed his legs back, my hands behind his knees and began doing just that.

"Yeah, oh yeah Matt, yeah! Mmmmmmmm..." he whispered, "Man you feel so good. Fuck me man, *fuck me Sir...*" I'd neither ordered him nor encouraged that moniker, it had simply happened honestly. We were both comfortable in the order of things. I jabbed and drilled into him deeper, sweat beginning to bead up on my forehead.

"Fuck yeah Dan, that's it. Open it up Boy, I'm ready..." He bucked and grabbed my butt cheeks, pulling me onto himself hard and tight. I felt his anus clench on my cock, and his dick oozed, then jumped and spurted thick white cum between and onto us. I gasped, growled and began to pump my own substantial load into his rectum, shooting massive gobs of my semen deep within his body. We grimaced, bucked and came together, then slid slowly into our embrace of post-coital intimacy.

Slowly kissing, I was about to back off, roll over, but Danny held me tightly, his asshole gripping my shaft as his hands held firmly on my rump. He didn't want me to remove myself; rather, he wanted me to complete the act of filling him.

"Do it man, give it to me," he breathed into my ear, all but inaudibly. "*Piss* in me, Sir. Give it to me, please! *Piss* in me, Sir! *Piss* in me..." I smiled and whispered back.

"Yeah boy, OK... Yes, here, I'll give it to you." In the darkness I relaxed my tube and slowly began to spurt my gold into his guts. I pumped, then forced the full stream up past his second sphincter. He rolled his eyes back, closing them as the sensation of hot piss filling his colon charged through his nerves. He gasped quickly, hotly, and I continued to piss.

"That's it, take it, take it," I mumbled, close and hot. "Take my *piss* Danny, here you go Boy... *mmmmmm* Ugggh...He pushed his pelvis upward, holding me as deep within himself as he could. I pumped and spurted, then gave him the last drops. It was done. We gazed into each other's eyes in wonder, in accomplishment.

Carefully pulling out of him, I rolled to my side and embraced him a long time, letting him simply float in the sensuousness after our fucking. At last he began to back away, pulling himself up.

"Sir?"

"Um, yeah?"

"I'm sorry, but I can't hold this tonight. I just can't, I think..." and he got up. Stepping QUICKLY down the hallway, I heard him smack the seat down and plop onto the throne. There was an obscene gushing and splashing as a full pint and more shot out of his asshole, my *piss*. Laying back and waiting in the darkened bedroom, I grinned proudly as I listened.

We'd slept well, all things considered. We were both resigned to the parting. Danny had had time to reflect, to heal a bit, and we'd had time to share the intimacy and hot sex we both so craved. I'd taken him, a neurotic and introverted trucker and closet homosexual, and, as with Doug, he was far more secure now, far more 'out' about his sexuality, but moreover stable within himself. And, he'd learned the new joys of hot piss. *Piss...* he shared the Obsession.

"I'm never going to wash this strap," he said. "Never. It's the memorial of _you_..."

I smiled and kissed him. "Mine too, Danny. Never." I gave him a couple contact numbers in Florida and the 150 bucks I'd managed to scrape up; then we got ready and walked out to the car. In a short while we were back on the same concourse at the airport, only 2 gates further down. Sure enough, Doug and Dave were there to see him off. Good handshakes, some back-slapping, a hidden tear or two, and we watched that tall, lanky cowboy head up the jetway. He disappeared around the corner, and I turned to go. Dave spoke.

"Didn't you want to watch him take off?"

"No," I said, "He's gone. But he'll never be forgotten, you know." Dave chuckled at that trite comment, but he understood. We were ready to walk away when I spotted another fine young man gazing up the jetway. Medium height, muscled and fine with a trim goatee. His western boots and tight jeans showed a nice thick bulge. About 34-35 or so. His keys hung on his left hip. He then looked at us, and I winked. He lifted his carry-on and began to head onto the plane, and once more looked back at me.

Again I winked, nodded at him. "Go get 'em," I whispered, hoping Danny indeed would find someone just like this guy. Silently I wished them both all the best, and we turned and walked away from the gate.

Danny was gone.

HENNEPIN TRANSFER AND PLAYGROUND

Getting back to work, Doug and I went on with nothing really different between us, but there was a new security, stability to his work. The unspoken connection strengthened him greatly His reading improved, but I still had to double-check most of his log sheets. The summer wore on, Dave had just been in for his 5th lay-over with Doug. Dave had spent 3 days and nights with him, then headed back to Salt Lake. He'd not be back for 2 weeks or so. Doug was crestfallen, he always knew their time together wouldn't last. But somehow, it was enough for them both and we went on.

Glancing over the schedule for the upcoming day, I noticed that once again we had a timber-hauler from Superior coming in. No doubt a Chattanooga Lines driver would be pulling it. I'd still not heard back about the davit boom that had gone to Tucson on Danny's truck, and that might make things interesting. I was on the afternoon shift when this one finally showed up, around 3:00.

The driver turned out to be a big, swaggering, heavy-set oaf from Euless, TX, one of the most senior drivers from C.L. His tight, tight jeans showed off some substantial man-meat, pointed 'Puerto Rican Cockroach Killers' on his feet. The fancy stitching and colored, tooled leather spoke of a wanna-be; most truckers would never spend that kind of cash on a pair of boots to drive in.

He too had a fucked-up, badly stacked load. I pretended not to notice; apparently he hadn't either. He was full of swagger and bravado, heavy on the CB jargon and macho shit. I bet he looked real rough and tumble, real _straight_, while on his knees and sucking away at some hot, sweaty, nasty uncut trucker dick too... yeah, they all do.

He checked in with an attitude, flipping his lading sheets onto the counter in front of me. "Hey there, BOY, you gonna deal with this here stuff WHEN?"

I glanced at the papers and mumbled non-committally, and continued the sheet I was working on. He glared, shifting from one foot to another, then sneered, talking a little bit louder. "HEY, I wanna know when this crap is gonna be set so I can..." I cut him off. Somehow I _knew_ who I was dealing with, and the anger was already boiling up within me.

"LOOK, _ASSHOLE_... I don't know who the fuck you think you're talking to, but that will god-damn well be the last time you take that shitty tone of voice with ME, got it?"

He froze, literally stopped in his tracks for a second, then took a big step backward. "Hey man, hey, settle down! Just tryin' to get some idea you know, I gotta get back outta here soon as possible you know. We're a driver short running the Tucson link."

I snorted some 'official-speak' about the manifest, the lading sheets and I'd be getting him going just as quick as I could, and oh by the way you got 7 ahead of you... it'll be a 'little while.' I figured if this jerk was who I thought he was, those other trucks might well take nigh on to 3 or 4 hours each... you never can tell, can you? I checked the sheets quickly: Duluth to Tucson, blah blah picking up blah blah at Hennepin Transfer, then on the road again. Destination: Davis-Monthan. Driver, William Wendell. Hmmm.

"Meanwhile _Wendell_, get your chunky ass back on that rig and move it off my turning apron; we've got equipment coming out of the mechanical shops." He swung off the step and backed away from the booth, then stomped back to his truck. He got in and pulled towards the parking areas directly ahead of me. The rig rolled to my right, about 100 yards, then began to swing left, completing about a 120 degree turn and heading onto the gravel at an angle. The main apron dropped off pretty sharply into the graveled area, sloping down a net drop of about 4 feet very quickly.

I watched him wobble and buck, the trailer shaking, and then... it swung farther, farther and just as I realized what was happening, the whole load shifted. Logs just below the top of the load creaked and slipped, then the changed center of gravity took the whole thing over to the right.

With a mighty crash of splitting timber, shattering wood and creaking steel flatbed, he lost it. The tandem did not break away and yup, the trailer dragged the cab right with it, flopping the whole mess onto its side right there in front of God and everyone. Screw 'God;' it was in front of 20 or 25 other truckers, that was by FAR the better deal. I screamed, roared aloud, "*HOLY SHIT*!" and then collapsed into a gibbering, laughing, hooting heap laying on the desk. I figured the jerk couldn't be too badly hurt, if at all. But *that* was pure Karma, serendipity in beautiful application.

Men were running thither and yon, guys were hemmin' and hawing, running to pull Wendell from the cab, trying to see what if anything anyone could do about the lost load. I got myself under control. I had to go survey it too. Mike Wales was coming down from the administration level with the office twats; waitresses, dishwashers, mechanics, pump jockeys, customers and other drivers ran in all directions. It was utter pandemonium, utterly wild!

I, however, was already formulating a plan of action. Mike got to the shaken-up driver, who was assuring everyone he was not injured. That kind of embarrassment is so glorious, satisfying and wonderful when such a pompous ass gets a comeuppance. It took awhile, but at last things got back to order. The wreck would have to remain where it was, at least for the time being. Mike and Wendell were conferring beside the office; I came up quietly, as much to eavesdrop as to offer anything.

"Well, we can help you get it all back together bud, we'll get a couple operators and a cherry picker. We'll get it all put back up proper like..." Mike was offering.

Then I reminded him that our extra boom had not been returned.

"Last I heard, that was leased out as temp fix for a fucked load up to get 'em outta here." I explained. "Guess they never sent it back. Say Mike, remember the memo I gave you about that?" He nodded.

Wendell started making noises about how stupid a way to run an operation that is, blah blah. Why the hell don't we have basic stuff, etc. and how long is it going to take to get some equipment and get me stacked up? That kind of shit.

"Well, I dunno man; I gotta check things out. Gimme a second and I'll be right back." Heading into the booth, I motioned Doug to come and help me, he was with me in seconds. Mike and Wendell went into the coffee shop to chill out.

He was concerned, worried for the driver. He hadn't seen the tip-over, only the aftermath. "He gonn' be OK, Doc? You check him out?" I laughed a bit.

"Yeah Doug, I did. Indeed. He's from Texas you know... Useless, TX. and one of Chattanooga Lines *very* finest. Top driver in fact." I let the thought trail away. "Will. William Wendell..." It didn't mean anything to him. Yet...

"Doug, can you give Dave a call? Get ahold of him if you need to?" He looked surprised.

"Yeah, I guess so... but his wife," I cut him off.

"Won't be anything to get you in dutch. I need him to tell me something. Tell us some _one_ that is." Doug was confused. "Call him, tell him to call me here in about an hour." Doug shrugged and went to do it.

I pulled the record from Danny's visit, his last trucking run. The lading sheets, the equipment list, all the names and dates. I went into the coffee shop. Mike had left the table but Wendell remained, still embarrassed. I sat and began to explain our dilemma.

"Well you see Will, it was in fact one of your Chattanooga trucks took our equipment down to Arizona. Um, yeah the Davis-Monthan transfer, you know?" He nodded. I went on.

"That driver was a... Dan something. Yeah, Dan Meinrad. Nice guy. He had a fucked-up load like you come in here with. We restacked him cause <u>Chatt</u> couldn't get him help until 2 days later or some stupid shit." Mike rejoined us. "That was the load where the second driver was fixin' to _die_ on us, remember Mike?" Indeed he did.

"Geez yeah. Will, _this_ is the guy saved that old man's life you know." Will was impressed. I shook my head.

"Nah, was more Danny did it. He came to get me or that guy woulda died. Anyhow... we sent the boom down to Tucson and nobody from Chatt Lines ever sent it back. Dan Meinrad got down there and I guess someone beat him up. Said he was a homo, beat him up and they kept our stuff..." Will didn't exactly choke on his coffee, but it was subtle, weird. Mike didn't catch it; I sure as hell did, and it proved my suspicion.

"Well..." he started. "I heard something about that; he got into a scrape with another driver and they let him go. I guess that had to be the mix up. You know, Chatt will send anything we need here, I just gotta get on the horn and make them get to it you know?" Suddenly he thought it was all <u>their</u> responsibility, not mine. I wasn't convinced. But now he was all business there, by gum, and yup it didn't matter whose fault things were, shit happens and we're all in this together and he'll just bite the bullet and take care of it. Sure.

"Um Mike, you know... they've sent at least two loads in here stacked like that. Dan's woulda been a dumper too but <u>he</u> was a good enough driver to SEE it." I punctuated that comment perfectly, Will winced. "And now *this* one went over in our lot, we're gonna be fucked up for at least a day from it. I think we damn well better make sure of safety compliance before it leaves. Make sure <u>ourselves</u>." Mike was nodding, agreeing. He wasn't on to what the deal was, but he knew there was a reason I wanted to fuck with Wendell and Chattanooga. He'd be curious to know why, meanwhile he'd go along with it.

And when he learned what had happened, he'd be more than glad to help me get even, if I needed anything. My plan was beginning to take shape already though.

Wendell was still trying to figure out how to proceed. He had to try to save face and stay at the forefront, but also agree with everything and be oh-so-cooperative, you know.

"Oh yes, well, we're sure going to have to review how things are being done up at Duluth. I'd checked it out, but you know, timber can shift. Can happen... we're just gonna have to make sure it doesn't happen again."

I huffed a bit. "Oh yes; indeed <u>we</u> will. Mike I think we're going to have to review our procedures with all timber haulers." Superior and Chattanooga were 'all.' "This is three I <u>know</u> of. God only knows how many other lop-side-ass loads Chatt's pulled in here that I <u>didn't</u> see." Mike glanced at me with real concern when I laid that one on him; and it was true, regardless of me fucking with Wendell.

"I'll have some recommendations for you tomorrow." We broke up the meeting, and I went back to the control booth. Doug was waiting.

"He'll be calling in a few minutes for you, what's up anyhow?" I smiled.

"I just wanna ask him for a couple references, that's all. Need a big strong driver I can talk to about something special." Doug was confused, but waited.

"Man, that Wendell... he's the one you know."

"What?"

"The fat ugly faggot that beat up Danny. That's 'what'." Doug whistled low.

"No shit?" I nodded, and the phone rang. I spoke low, quickly, but Dave gave me what I needed in a matter of seconds. Doug had already called in our operators, and we'd have the timber hauler up and ready around midnight, meanwhile I wanted not only to sweat Wendell, but get things ready. I had a list of particular trucks, drivers I might find. I went out to see who was on the yard.

George Bakersfield was *it*. Woof! Maybe 38, he stood six-six and about 260, ripped muscles, hairy bod, a full beard and killer eyes. A real man's man and not at all reticent when it came to wild, intimate action with other woofy truckers. Bake was about as 'out' as it was possible to be in those days. He was up in a big, sparkling new rig from English Freight: maroon trimmed with chrome, chrome, chrome and some new chrome. He waved me in.

I explained in very few sentences what the deal was, what I suggested doing. He smiled with an evil glint in his eye and agreed with some fake hesitance.

"You're gonna owe me a big one on this, pal." I smiled and nodded quickly.

"Goes around, comes around George, that's the whole fuckin' point."

He sat back, pondering and grinning.

"Leave it to me."

"Yeah man, I just want you to include that detail, OK?" He wondered about it, then agreed.

"I ain't never done that, but alright."

I mocked a TV commercial "*Try it, you'll LIKE it!*" He laughed. "Really, you will. It's hot."

I clambered back down, and got back to work. Doug was dying to know what was going on, but I didn't say much. Only that he might wanna stick around and have a late dinner with me, be in the coffee shop around 11:00 or so.

The forklift and crane operators salvaged what they could of the timber load. Most of it was surprisingly intact; the scrap would be taken up by workers demolishing an old truck shop on the back forty. Their equipment and office trailers had just been brought in to our facility. The trailer was damaged, but a state inspector signed off for it. They'd loaded it up and Wendell could be back on the road in a few hours.

Wendell was nowhere to be seen. Neither was George Bakersfield... I would've liked a film of what I knew was transpiring, but we hadn't agreed to that. Nor did I have the 5 grand or so it would've taken. Had we had a pile of cash, I'd bet George actually <u>would</u> have made a film of it, too! Doug and I finished our shift, and turned things over to Larry and Phil ('Moe,') the new guys. I'd wondered if there was something going on between those two; they were awfully insistent upon teaming together. But they also acted like punk dopers or something. Who cared? They got the job done.

We chose a corner booth in the restaurant and ordered some supper. The coffee bar in the center of the room had 6 or 7 truckers seated, and there were 5 or so other tables going, maybe 20 men all told. George came in and seated himself not far from us, but did not acknowledge me. He grabbed his menu and ordered coffee. Our food arrived and Will Wendell came in, adjusting his belt and glancing around. He walked directly to George's booth and slid in. They ordered and in a few minutes food came.

I waited expectantly, and then it started. George looked across his table with disgust and chided Will, just a *little bit* too loud.

"Jesus man, don't be touching the sugars and stuff!" Will was shocked, but didn't catch on yet. He mumbled something low, smiling, maybe hinting about what the two of them had been doing. George scowled and paused, waiting for the next opportunity.

"Hey fucker! Fuckin' *pig*, you been *drinkin' my piss* with that mouth, keep your damn fork away from my plate!" Two of the guys at the coffee bar snapped their heads around, staring at these guys. Wendell was shocked, horrified, and tried *quietly* to calm George down, *quietly*... Bake wasn't having it.

"Oh no shit? You just get into that stuff long as nobody thinks you *like* it huh? Sure, you looked real fuckin' tough with my dick up your ass..." He mocked Wendell's characteristic twang.

"*Yeah daddy, gimme that Superior Timber ('tayim-ber,') gimme that LOG up my ass man!*" I thought the trucker nearest me was going to explode laughing. His face began to turn a bright shade of crimson; so did Will Wendell's. George added one more thought.

"The piss-pigs usually hang out up in that small john upstairs, the one with only one stall. I ain't never knowed anyone who drank it in *HIS OWN TRUCK*..." George said clearly, to the room. Wendell's mind and pride snapped.

"YOU FUCKING BASTARD! I'LL KILL YOU!" and tried to reach

across the table. George flung the table aside, dishes and cups, food, silverware and all, and they were on their feet. Wendell's slick boots didn't help and he slid just a few inches, his balance was destroyed. He'd actually have been almost a match for Bakersfield, but George had the intent and the upper edge. He swung and connected hard; Wendell went down.

"YOU MOTHERFUCKER! You fucking lying BASTARD! FUCKING BASTARD!" Wendell yelled, insane with humiliation and pain. George stepped quickly aside and waited; I knew were this not staged, he'd've already given the second and final hit. He waited for Will to rise. "FUCKING LIAR! MOTHER FUCKING LYING BASTARD!"

George swung again, and I could tell it was not a real, full punch, but packed enough force that with the shame factor, Will went down again, blubbering in hot anger, humiliated and destroyed. He was trying valiantly to hold back his tears, and then Bakersfield fired the *coup de grace*.

"Get the hell outta here pig, before my fucking SPERM soils your panties!" He stepped back.

George smiled, glancing around the room. The shock and amazement on every face in there was a sight to behold. Doug sat across from me, utterly dumbfounded. Will Wendell was on his hands and knees, his head hanging down, bloodied and hot, desperate tears running freely. There wasn't a sound; you could've heard a cotter-pin drop...

Bake reached into his back pocket and pulled out a wallet. With a gesture of utter contempt he handed the waitress a $50 bill and turned on his heel. He left.

At long last, Wendell managed to lift himself from the floor. He stood, not meeting anyone's gaze. The other men in the room gave him no quarter. The eyes of all were upon him, expressions flat, blank, inscrutable, cold and filled with judgment and condemnation. He glanced at us, then once around the room. With painful steps he finally walked away, out of the room. Through the large windows we could see him heading back to his truck, his head down. He walked like someone who'd been through an airplane crash or a building collapse. Handicapped beyond description but trying to get away... I smiled.

Doug was still unable to react, his mouth hanging open, his fork dangling from his hand, a clump of salad stuck on the tines. I smiled and spoke.

"That's how you play '*Getting Even*'," I said, loud enough for everyone to hear. A burly bearded driver at the coffee bar, chuckled, then snickered. Then laughed, and was quickly joined by more. The room exploded in fierce, brutal laughter. Maybe they didn't know <u>why</u> it'd been done, but the idea it had been deserved pleased them all. Their laughter was to relieve their own tension, a catharsis; behind it, as with Doug, there was the element of deep shame and self-consciousness. The sense that it could've happened to many of them, *any* of them. And they knew it, too.

The busboy was sent to clean up the room and we decided to skip eating. Doug wasn't able, and I had only gone in there for the show. I paid up and we headed back to the operations booth. Doug said nothing until we were out on the walkway; we could see the cab lights were burning in the Chattanooga Lines cab, its engine rumbling loudly. But Wendell had the curtains up, hiding his shame.

"Damn Matt, fucking DAYUMM... you *destroyed* him...!" Doug was disgusted. I turned to him with anger, my eyes flashing.

"What goes around comes around Doug. He likes to air shit in public? Well howdy-ho, let *him* fucking try it on for size!"

"You didn't have to do that..." he said softly. He looked across the concrete to our control booth.

"That's just it Doug. *I* didn't *do* anything. HE DID." Larry was glancing out the door, as yet unaware of events. "*His* actions Doug; just like in Tucson." I paused.

"What if the first time Dave had been with you, he turned over and called *Wendell* to come and see it, to laugh at and mock what *you* thought was private, was yours and his?" Doug pondered; he was putting the shoe on the other foot. He began to nod slowly.

"Well that's what he did to Danny! And now he knows what that kind of bullshit feels like, right up to the knock-down drag-out in public. And we'll see what Chattanooga Lines thinks about him parading their colors, huh?"

Doug's sympathetic nature still held him, but he had to agree. He smiled, chuckled.

"God-DAMN Matt... I'm glad you're on my side!" I smiled bitterly as I returned to the booth, and Doug went home for the night.

I stayed at the terminal through the night, telling Larry and 'Moe' that the Chattanooga dumper deal was my baby. I'd make sure everything was chilly and kosher before he left, and make sure all was straight with the company. Moe was happy to let me take the shift and scooted out. The C.L. truck still rumbled in the lot; Wendell had not emerged since the show. The phone rang at 4:40 AM.

"Um, this is Jim Jameson," the caller identified himself. I'd never talked to the Chattanooga Lines owner before, and was real polite. "You got a hauler there who's had a mishap I understand? Has he left the facility?"

"Mr. Jameson, no, he's still here. I'm the ops manager; I supervised reloading that mess. This was worse than the one last month." He grunted; he'd not known about the other situation. I elaborated.

"Yeah, one of your other drivers had the same thing, but he'd sat tight and made sure he was stable before trying to pull around. You oughtta see if you can't get that guy. Goddam good hauler..." Jameson seized the opportunity to make it all go away.

"OK sure, I'll round him up; if he's one of ours, I'll get him there ASAP. You remember who it was?"

Now it was my turn. "Damn right I do. He's the one some fat fuck got fired in Tucson; Danny Meinrad is his name. I dunno where you're gonna find him now." That was the last straw. Jameson said something about finding a qualified driver to take the load; could _I_ park it till they worked it out?

"You're that new ground manager, right? Will _you_ go do it? Twenty-four hours, tops. I'll find you a driver and find him now."

I assured him I'd pull the rig to the side apron myself; Mr. Jameson was gracious and thanked me. Oh and by the way, would I mind giving Wendell a message? I readily agreed.

"We'll wire his trip pay; tell him he gets the miles from Duluth to Hennepin, and that's all. We can't have a driver who dumps his load like that on our team..." He continued, trying to save his own face for that matter. "He's had some other mishaps, it's too bad. He was a good hauler in his day."

"So was Meinrad. So _is_ Dan Meinrad," I snarled. Jameson knew what I was hinting, and I knew they'd track Danny down with an offer before this kind of shit got aired up in a Minnesota courtroom or news paper. Bad trucker, dumped load, liability in the yard, previous incident and an unjust firing; and all of it with that beautiful homo-twist. Get rid of it... I went to the teletype to wait for the documents, then took them out to Wendell's truck. I played sympathetic.

"Well, I'm sorry man, but this just came in. I guess the boss can't handle controversy you know... makes the company look bad." He was deadpan, still in shock. He took the print-out and looked at it.

"Man, you didn't believe that shit that fucker was goin' on about, did you?" I could barely keep from degenerating into hysterical laughter.

"Oh no man, he's a whacko, everyone knows that! No man, nobody _believed_ that stuff. No one..." He wanted to buy it; he pretended, told himself it was so.

"Yeah OK... it's cool." His face was coloring nicely from the two punches he'd taken. I wanted him to know who and why it had happened, but maybe that would go through the pipeline later. Right now, I didn't dare let on. Chickenshit, maybe; stupid, no.

I told Wendell he could have a couple hours to clear out his gear, make some arrangements. Then I got back out, and cruised the parking area. I found the English truck and George Bakersfield. He wasn't sure if he was happy with himself or not. But he agreed: _that_ comeuppance was way overdue. He'd been acquainted with Wendell in the past. I grinned at him and sat on the passenger side.

"So, when you gonna give me your pay-off?" he asked. "You know what I'm gonna take..." I nodded.

"George, after that, you do what you like. Any time." He smiled.

"You're gonna get it rougher than he did you know..."

"Buddy, do what you want. I'll make it worthwhile. You want me to get crazy, hell... put me up on the loading dock and I'll drink your piss in front of the whole troop, then fuck me as rough as you can. That was worth it."

"Hahaha, maybe next time I'm here," he laughed. "I gotta kinda lay low myself now you know... Maybe next time."

"Let me know fucker; my ass is yours!" I opened the door to leave. He stopped me one last time.

"*Hey!.*" I turned back, my foot on the lower step, my eyes questioning.

"You owe me a $50 bill!"

THE BACK FORTY

George took his 'payment' the next week. Once more I had to laugh, thinking of Bre'r Rabbit. *Oh no! Don't throw me in that briar patch!* He spotted me in the office around two, but I wasn't able to get out of there until I'd taken care of an illiterate black driver from Biloxi, Mississippi. The guy had been infuriating; how that kind of man could ever get a CDL was beyond me, as the simplest concepts of truck operation and freight hauling seemed to be a complete mystery to him. His paperwork was a nightmare, but at last he was on his way and I headed out to the yard.

George saw me walking up, and tooted his air horn. He motioned me up into his truck and grinned.

"You ready?" he asked. He didn't mince any words and he didn't waste any time. "I need to bust a nut man. Besides, I been wanting to part your ass-cheeks for awhile now."

"Well shit, all ya hadda do was say so, bud," I answered. He laughed.

"Get them jeans off man, get on the bunk and grease up." I stepped to the back of the cab and found supplies. I was quickly on my back and ready. Bake closed the main curtain and was with me a second later, his hot cock standing at attention. It rose almost straight upward, touching his navel as it pulsed and waited.

He moved atop me, quickly, but not hurriedly. He was surprisingly gentle, his fat dick sliding into me with a slow, inexorable pressure. My guts and asshole sang as he split me, probing almost 8 inches up my ass. Holding my legs apart, he began a very sensuous, deep prostate massage, sliding into me to the hilt, then pulling back slowly and firmly. I'd never felt anything like his back-stroke, it felt as though there was a kind of suction, his cock pulling my tube outward, until the head of his cock was actually outside me. Only the very tip of his slit remained within my anus, then he reversed and slid back in, in again.

On and on the slow, beautiful stroking went. He picked up the pace, but for me the matter was one of total sensation. It wasn't wild and frantic, but the hairy man, his fat, fat dick and pure horny masculinity was incredible. My cock throbbed, pumped up as hard as I've ever felt it, rubbing on his hairy abdomen. He took his time, enjoying the feeling of my asshole and the full contact of his length within me.

On it went, almost no talking, not from embarrassment or reticence, but there simply was no need. We enjoyed the hot fucking: his cock, my asshole. He began to pump a bit faster, harder, and I knew his load would soon be the pay-off. *What a way to even up an obligation*, I thought! I spread my ass a bit wider, letting him mash his nuts against the base of my buttocks, forcing him into myself a bit deeper.

He bucked, pushed in fully, and gritting his teeth, simply poured his molten cum up inside me. I felt it, the temperature of his cum was far above that of his body; or perhaps of my body. It was warm, thick and satisfying. I grabbed his hairy ass-cheeks and held him hard within me, stroking my own cock until the cum began to spurt thickly onto our bellies.

"Yeah buddy, cum with me, yeah *with* me, *with* me. Oh fuck yeah!" he mumbled, enjoying it completely. He pressed me back, open farther and watched as the last of my seed spurted up and out. We sank into a sweaty heap and lay there.

With a slow tug, George removed his deflating cock from me, and got up from the bunk. He stood, his fine body framed in the back-lighted glow of afternoon sun, filtering through the curtains. He motioned to me.

"Mmmmm, come on down here buddy. I wanna give you the rest." He smiled. "I gotta agree, since you told me to give it to that Wendell guy." I grinned.

"Yeah man, I told you you'd like it, huh?" I got onto the floor in front of him, and waited for him to give some direction. He took a stance, and wiped his cock with his T-shirt. I reached up and pulled that fine meat just into my mouth, and slid it back and forth, slicking him up. He pulled back a bit, taking what was also my favorite position. His cockhead was just into my lips, the slit poised at the tip of my tongue.

He groaned, paused and waited. The anticipation for this hot man's load was beautiful, I knew it would be fantastic. It wasn't long in beginning, and I hadn't been mistaken. He shifted a bit, and that first salty droplet formed in his slit and dribbled into my waiting, thirsty mouth.

I sucked and pulled it from him, then the head of his cock flared, pulsated and opened wide. A thick hot stream began to shoot into me and I gulped.

Piss, his piss began to feed me.

I placed my hands up on his lower belly, worshipping as a suppliant. He pissed hot and hard then, and I had to gulp and swallow quickly, fully to keep up with him. I cupped his balls in my hand and he moaned low in pleasure.

"Mmmmm, yeah buddy, that's it. Mmmmm, that feels nice, hold me there boy and take it, yeah that's it." He spoke low and clearly, his voice beautiful in his simplicity and fondness of hot male sex, hot, hot *piss*. I drank on.

The stream flowed and I ached in pleasure taking it, my own cock thick and hard in my jockstrap. I felt a twinge and despite my clenching, his spunk leaked out my asshole and went running into my jock as I fed on his cock, on his piss. *Piss*, oh god. I was taking piss from the hottest, finest driver on the yard! He fed me in pure, uninhibited pleasure, his elation at giving it matched only by my obsession with taking it, draining him, taking him inside me, consuming his Essence.

He whispered to me, "Yeah buddy, yeah fucker, goddam that's fine. Man I like this; take it now, here's more." He spurted, I felt his dick jump and flex, then another full hot stream coursed into my gullet. I swallowed, almost choked, but held onto him. I sucked, drank and loved it. The beautiful flow trailed off abruptly, then he was done, One last short pulse of salty goodness finished his load.

I had drained him. He smiled.

"Yeah buddy, wow. Good work!" He ran a thick, powerful hand on the back of my head, pawed me and pulled away.

"Damn man, it's after four, I gotta get this crap ready to go." He turned to the pile of paperwork and junk on his dashboard. Our sexual coupling over, I was dismissed. I dressed quickly. But as I opened the door to leave, he looked up once more.

"Think you might stop by after you punch out, dude? I gotta get some dinner, drink a few cups of coffee you know... maybe go for another round?"

I chuckled. "Sure thing man, you got it. Around 10:30; fuck me all you like buddy. I'll be *thirsty* by then too."

"YEAH! Good deal. See you then."

The evening meeting was move for move, moment for moment virtually a repeat of the first one; but totally satisfying for us both. He pulled out of the terminal and headed back on the road at midnight, and the season went on.

––––––––––––

Danny Meinrad stopped in a couple times. Jim Jameson had offered him to return to work, even gave him some back pay. He'd taken it, then dumped Chattanooga Lines high and dry as soon as he was back in the groove. He took his certifications to Florida, and was living with a driver from Wyoming, a real honest-to-goodness cowboy, and a fine man. They team-drove, and it was more satisfying than anything to see them happy, horny and <u>together</u>. He always had a big smile and a good, tight hug for me.

The season had gone into fall, then winter. The heaps of snow are always an issue in Minneapolis in January; we had plows and operators, and kept things going. I saw to it that we had not a single major snow delay in early 1979. I'd been promoted thrice, and was junior only to Mike Wales. Now I had the title (and the <u>pay</u>) for managing all operations on the ground, not just the responsibility and the bullshit.

February became March, and I was still working my 'summer job,' having not responded to acceptances for graduate school. I'd put it off a year, maybe two. I had another birthday, and the first really nice day of the year found the contractors back on the job, setting up the back forty to clear it for a new truck-wash facility.

They had several trailers: one for offices, 3 for tool and equipment storage, and one was set up as a worker's lounge. Some of their guys were even hotter than the truckers, better bodies and they stayed out in the open all day, sweating and showing off. Some great eye-candy, and of course having to do go-fer business with and for them was a chore I didn't mind at all. Nope, not at all.

I was restless, afflicted with spring fever and not at all into working in that fucking booth. Everyone was. I walked out to see how things were going on the construction site. Within seconds I'd run into the very man out there I'd most hoped to see.

John Hernandez was from California, half Mexican and half Anglo. His fine, smooth brown skin was offset by the most beautiful blue, piercing eyes, and his groomed facial hair was stunning. His muscles stood out in masculine knots, curves on his shoulders, around his ass, up his back, down his chest. Oh God, on and on! A puka-shell necklace was his only adornment. He wore it well, but truthfully his body didn't need extra ornamentation.

I caught up to him and struck up a conversation. "Hey Juan! How ya doing? I asked. He smiled a bit. I'd learned that many guys called him 'Juan;' he often didn't like it, but it was reserved for pals. Doug and I were OK using it, Mike Wales and others were not. "Bored with work this FINE fuckin' day?" He grinned and nodded.

"Man don't you know it! I can't get into this shit at all!" His jeans enveloped fine equipment, curves on curves on curves, yet somehow angular, masculine. His keys hung on his right belt-loop, a navy blue bandanna in his left pocket. Interesting. Might not mean anything at all. But then again, it might... A glint of gold caught my eye, gleaming on his hand. A wide plain band, a wedding band, but on his right hand. REAL interesting... I wondered at it, as I was all but certain he was one who went for a little man-fun from time to time.

I shifted my weight, my own bulge showing nicely. He glanced down carefully, but I noticed his gaze travel up from my boots, lingering on my basket just long enough, just long enough. Yup. He looked me up and down then in 'regular guy' fashion. I smiled, and subtly posed again. "I got a couple beers on ice man, what say we just knock off and enjoy them?" He smiled.

"Well yeah, but my foreman is here, I can't just go off drinking." I chuckled and said I needed him to check up on some stuff with me at the office. We went back to the booth.

Larry had it all running smoothly; Moe was no longer his team mate. I didn't hear the details but I'd gotten the idea that Moe had wanted more than just being buddy-buddy and working together, and Larry wasn't having it. They'd parted on OK terms, but parted. He now had some babe named 'Treesa' working with him. We called her 'Curly.' She was cool too, they got it done. I picked up the in-house phone and got Mike Wales on the line. John waited.

"Yeah Mike, that foreman is here today, he's got that crap about the water lines to the new pump-house you know? Maybe you wanna talk to him? Schmidt is out there too." I meant the general contractor, who had all the spec sheets and blueprints for their project.

Mike grunted something about sending them up to his office ASAP. I walked halfway to the edge of the back-field property with John and told him to send the other two up to Mike; I'd join him shortly with the cooler. He grinned.

"Oh, *si si, Señor!*" he said, giggling at his own Mex imitation. He'd gone to UCLA; he was far from being a stupid wetback, but could sure play one if and when it suited him. A minute later the head honchos were going up to Mike's office and I was opening the shabby tool trailer. The door and windows were on the back side, hidden from any and all views. I shoved the cooler up into it and Juan was at my side.

"C'mon man, let's chill out!" I said, and he smiled again. It seemed to me his bulge was that much more pronounced. Mine definitely was. He closed the door behind us, and locked it from inside.

A sleazy old couch sat long one wall, a 12' work-table on the other. Boxes of miscellaneous crap were here and there, but for the most part the trailer was empty. It was damn near the size of a full semi-trailer. We sat on the couch and I pulled up a can of beer for each of us. We took a long deep chug, and Juan sat, his legs apart, pointing his stuff at me. He smiled. We drank the first one quickly, making deliberately inane small-talk. We opened the second can. He took about half of it in one slug; I emulated.

"I don't really care for more beer right now..." he said, and ran his hand up his own thigh, just below his nuts. I grinned, and set my Bud on the floor.

"Me either man. Better idea...?" and stood, my bulge only a foot from his face. He reached over and stroked me, gripping my cock through the work pants. He rose up to meet me, and quickly I'd joined him tongue to tongue, our slobbering kisses hot and deep. I mashed my body against his, he responded with thrusts and grinding of his own. His hands grabbed my ass, kneading me through my clothing.

"Yeah buddy, this is what we need," he groaned, and began to yank my belt open. I responded and we were soon out of our boots and jeans, open shirts hanging above our naked, raw masculinities. I leaned it to slurp and chew his fine nipple as he continued to knead and work my ass, probing with a hot finger, pushing past the straps of my jock. My asshole twitched, clenching on his finger as he thrust in deeper, pressing on the back of my gland. I oozed and reached for his cock.

He was uncut, thick and brown. The smoothness of his body continued onto his dick, his shaft barely showing a vein at all. Mine stood out hot and hard, the blood vessels pumping blue and red up and down and into my sac. I flicked a gob of precum from his slit, then took it up to my mouth to taste him. I stroked him and nestled his balls, provoking a low groan.

He leaned back, his hand on my butt, and then pulled me close and down. I knelt as he thrust this hot dick into my face, then opened my mouth. With a slipping jab, he buried himself to the root. I gulped, almost choking. Beer foam welled up but I sucked and held him tight.

"Yeah man, go for it!" he said. "Yeah suck that dick buddy, suck me..."

John ground his nuts onto my chin, and reached below them to pull them up, mashing them firmly in place. His cock reached the back of my throat and probed; I held him by the ass-cheeks and pulled him in deeper, sucking madly. Slobber ran down the corner of my mouth, onto my chin, and dribbled onto the floor. Slicking him up, I slobbered more and more. He was ready.

He pulled me up, then motioned to the couch. "Yeah OK," I said softly, "however you like."

"Aw man, hot... on your knees ok?" I complied, spreading nice and wide. He spat a gob of mucous onto his fingers and lubed me. Taking aim on my hole, he touched me slightly, just pushing into the ring. Then a hot hard shove and half his 7" were buried in my ass.

"Ugggh, yeah man, lemme have it! Go ahead man, hard as you like, I can take it!" I encouraged him. With that, he put some 'ummmph' into it and began to fuck in earnest. Shoving himself into me 'til our balls knocked together we started to buck and fuck, the trailer responding with an almost imperceivable rocking. I arched forward, holding the backrest of the old couch, bucking back to meet his thrusts in counterpoint. Juan groaned.

"Ummm fuck yeah buddy, take it. Yeah! Oh man, yeah that's it!" he egged me on, low and horny. Our bodies joined in hot union and his cockhead reached up into me. My dick flopped and leaked, hanging from the side of my strap. He jacked me as he drilled, giving me a hot reach-around. We creaked and rocked in tandem, his hard thick shaft probing into me with lusty jabs.

It was not long lasting; within a few short minutes John's cockhead was swelling within my tunnel. He bucked again, his low moan becoming hotter and louder. With a hard thrust, he drilled into me deep, holding me tight in his embrace as his dick exploded cum inside me.

"Agggh yeah man, yeah I'm cumming man! Uuugggggh!" He pulled back and began hot short thrusting, going back and forth wildly, as his spunk shot in thick gobs just within my asshole-ring. He stroked back and forth, hot and hard, using his own cum to grease the way.

For long seconds after he'd shot, Juan kept the hot, short stroke going, fucking in his own load. I was relaxed totally, my asshole dripping his cum while he still fucked me. My cock jumped, oozed, aching for relief, but as his orgasm dwindled, he wasn't interested in my dick. He pulled back and away, leaving my dripping fuck-hole used and raw, empty.

"Aw yeah fucker! Yeah!" he grunted, and flopped onto the couch beside me. I sat back on the seedy, dirty upholstery beside him. He made no move to assist me getting off. I stroked myself idly. He wasn't done though; he leaned back far, thrusting his cock upward as the thick spunk globbed on the sides of his meat glimmered and shone in the light. His hand was on the back of my neck as I jacked myself.

I licked and slurped on his cock, taking up the salty cream coating him. That funky taste of ass-juices mixed with cum was hot, wild and horny. My dick throbbed as I approached the line, ready to shoot hard and far. Juan humped upward though, and his firm grip slowed me. He needed something else...

Sucking on his cock, I slowed and waited as he relaxed. He whispered suggestively. "Man, I could use a little bit more... just a little something more, OK?" Dropping my own hard cock to attend him, I slid my hand up his thigh and rubbed lightly on his balls. The sac tightened, pulling them into his body closely. He moaned again.

Without saying a word, I encouraged his thought. He moved slightly, getting himself a bit more comfortable, more accessible. I nursed on his dickhead and he closed his eyes, floating in post-orgasm and let himself begin. His slit flared, the edge of his foreskin wrapped around the base of his corona. A salty burst, hot and redolent, pulsed onto my tongue. Then a flood gushed up into my waiting, thirsty mouth.

Piss. Hot salty golden piss.

I gulped, taking it down. A hot, heavy gush shot up into my gullet, overwhelming me. I tried to back away, but John held me on his cock. Piss shot out from around his dick, out of my mouth and nostrils. He didn't flinch, it was what he'd intended, apparently. I sucked and slurped, taking more, as we wallowed in his yellow, hot piss. Piss, *mmmmm*, it was fine. Hot piss, salty and delicious flowed onto and around us both as I nursed from him. He groaned in pleasure, feeding me.

"Yeah man, that's it. Drink it buddy, yeah!" he whispered, and his stream shot hard and waned, hot and then slow. "Drink my piss, man!" His load tapered off, finished. I slurped a bit more, and he was done.

"Aw fuck yeah man, yeah... fuckin' piss drinker too, that's hot!" He smiled, and pulled his cock away from me. My penis oozed as I gripped it tightly. I began to jack again, reaching my own orgasm in seconds. I lay my face onto his piss-coated thigh, his hand still gripping me firmly at the nape of my neck.

"Ugggh, aw fuck John, fucker... I'm gonna shoot it, yeah!" and with hot spurts, my cum shot between us, splattering thickly onto his leg, on the front of the couch, on my body and hand. "Aggh fuck yeah!"

I spurted and blew my nuts, and began to sink down to relax. John was done though, and pushed me away, not roughly but unmistakably. I pulled back and rose with him.

He grabbed a gob of my cum, scraping it off his leg and smearing it onto the old sofa. "Yeah there, mark that fucker!" he laughed. I did likewise, smearing my jock too.

"Fuck yeah bro, that's what we needed!" He began to gather up his clothing, and quickly dressed himself, not hesitating to pull his garments over his piss-coated skin. So did I, and we got ourselves dressed in hot piss-lust. My cum was matted in my bush and body hair, his cum still leaking from my asshole; his piss scenting us both.

We sucked down the remainder of our beer as we got ready to get back out. With a click, the door was open and we headed back onto the construction site. He motioned to me to hold back, and stepped around one end of the trailer, heading away. In a few seconds he'd joined a couple other workers about 20 yards away, taking their break by one of the other office trailers. I heard them hailing one another, and turned to head the other way. I returned to the glass booth by the turning apron.

Larry was off getting some coffee, Curly was busy on the teletype. I checked over the paperwork on the counter, all seemed quite a-OK, and headed back into the main building. I had a change of clothes in a locker up in the shower area, and decided I'd better clean up before John's thick, salty piss gave me a rash. I was sorry to have to part with it.

STACKED FIVE HIGH

That week went quickly as we picked up the pace. To the regular volume of transfer traffic was added the suppliers and traffic and workers for the construction project. The foundation men were there as April began unusually hot and humid; *Concrete Workers Do It Harder*, you know. Yeah!

The strings were all in place, pallets of materials unloaded. The foundations had been clawed out by the earth-movers and the real work began. Two days of pouring, and the foundation and slab were in place with the long weekend to cure. Tuesday the following week saw the steel framing and carpentry begun, and within another week a building had taken shape. Cladding was going on, brickwork would follow. The place was a hive of activity, with woofy, hunky men from one end of the lot to the other.

On a very hot afternoon in late April, I went out to survey the progress. I walked around the site, from the edge of our old transfer lots out to the new facility. Soon the whole of the acreage would be paved, joined up in one seamless functioning truck center. But now I walked on dirt, gravel and dried, struggling weeds. As I got back to the office trailers, two big concrete men spattered with gray material were standing and chatting beside a pile of hand-equipment. The shafts of their big trowels and a nasty bent-up wheelbarrow sat idle, the guys laughed and gesticulated. I checked them out as I approached.

One called to me; I could see they had thermoses beside them, but I was pretty sure it was not coffee they were drinking. I hailed them in reply, and walked up.

They were dirty, hot and sweaty. One had dark hair and a thick, thick beard; his eyes brown behind medium-grade sunglasses. He buddy was smallish, but well formed, his pecs and biceps bulging in a tight, form-fitting blue T-shirt. He flexed a bit for me, enjoying my discreet admiration.

"Hey buddy, what's up with this crap today huh?" the big guy asked. "We sure can't do anything out here. Doesn't seem like the crew should be working today though. We're not gonn' get the side lot strung out till that crap is done. Guess we're gonna play around till we can actually work, huh?" He laughed, not smashed but nicely oiled.

I huffed some vague agreement and they offered me a cup from their thermos. I accepted. It was strong, vodka and some fruit punch mix, a lot of soda foaming in the brew. I sipped half my cup in quick time. They refilled me.

"Yup, just gonna kick back a couple days here," the small hunk was saying. Gary was his name; his pal was Rob. The sweat moistened them both, their scent thick and pungent. I tried to sniff at them without making it obvious, but Rob noticed. He lifted his arm and sniffed himself.

"Hot huh? Hehehe, yeah nothing like working up a good sweat, especially on the clock with nothing to do, huh?" He laughed wildly. His jeans creased across the front of his pelvis, filled with thick, beckoning man-meat. He lowered his arm and adjusted his belt, groping his basket. I smiled noncommittally. Gary posed and took another cupful of the cocktail, draining the container.

"Aw, that's that," he said. "What are we gonna do now?" He looked at Rob and then at me. "Maybe we should check out that office trailer, huh?" I wondered at the come-on. If Juan had said anything, I'd be surprised; but if he hadn't, the coincidence was kind of strange. And if he had and this was a set-up by these drunks to bash me, I was going to be in real trouble.

"Well I dunno about that man, I'm still working you know. Can't just drop it and go hide out for the day." Gary wasn't convinced, and Rob smacked him on the shoulder, hard.

"Yeah, Gary wants to go hide out all right. He wants to suck that big cock you're toting in them Carhartt's buddy!" He laughed. No, this was no set up. "Come on man, let's go get nasty!" Rob laughed and pitched his steel coffee mug into the wheelbarrow. "Whaddaya say? Wanna go fuck?" Gary watched me intently, suddenly totally sober.

"Um, well... how can I say 'no' to that kind of need?" I answered altruistically. ('*Honest, Mom, they needed to fuck. I had to do it...*') Gary laughed wildly.

"Yeah man, come on!" They spun toward the trailer and I followed, climbing in behind them. Gary was already opening the front of his Levi's, his damp fur sticking up in clumps. No drawers, just hot man flesh. Rob got behind me and groped my basket from around me while Gary began to undress me, my shirt, then belt. In a few seconds, we were all stripped down, the hot, stuffy trailer already reeking of man-sweat and sexual need. Rob's cock was *huge*, more than a full nine-incher. Thick and veiny, his knob glistened with sweat from riding in his tight work jeans. He wore a fine, sweaty *jockstrap*... I wished I'd kept mine on, but Gary had already yanked it down and off me.

Gary's dick was smaller, maybe 7" if that. But what he lacked in mass he made up for in power and hot hard horny heat. Rob slid his dick between my legs, up under my balls, and Gary dropped to his knees to suck me, yanking and tugging on his own dick as he got ready.

Rob held me firmly, leaning me onto his massive chest with my pelvis thrust forward, and Gary quickly took my substantial cock into his mouth. With a grunt, he jammed his face onto me, taking me to the root in a gulp. I moaned and Rob began to stroke his oozing cock against me, the hot cockhead jumping up, poking against my asshole, making me worry about the fullness of being penetrated by him.

Gary rose, and mashing himself onto the front of me, reached around to hold Rob by his cheeks. I was pressed between them, sandwiched. Gary stretched himself up to me, taking my tongue into his mouth and kissing me as Rob hugged me and stroked him. We broke the kiss off and Rob leaned over my shoulder, pulling Gary's face to himself. Over my shoulder they then sucked tongue, kissing and grunting. We began to sweat in profusion.

Rob pushed me forward a bit, his cock sticking to my thigh as he pulled it back; then he was in front of me and Gary was sandwiched. Again we humped and explored, kissing one another and then side by side, all 3 of us kissing in hot unison. Beards mingled, moustaches tangled, tongues slobbered and we shared it all. I stroked their cocks, holding both at once. Rob's massive, powerful hard-on leaked as I did. It was him who suggested sharing something else.

He moved me in front of him and pushed on my shoulders. I sank to suck him, and Gary was right beside him, determined not to miss out on the action. I tried to suck them both, but the disproportion was simply too much. Rob's meat just pushed Gary's beautiful cock aside. But Rob had more in mind anyway.

"Yeah man, suck me. That's it... suck it bro, Now here..." and without another sound or word, his valve opened and his piss gushed onto me, into my face, into my mouth. Piss, wild and free. I lurched myself forward to clamp my mouth over his spurting glans; Gary gasped in horny elation.

"OH FUCK! Yeah dude, take that hot fuckin' piss, go man!" he encouraged. Rob let it fly, soaking me thoroughly and letting me drink as I could. He wrapped his arm around Gary's waist and held him close beside himself, then egged him on as well.

"Come on man, let it go. It's ok buddy, give him your piss." He spoke with reverence, his obsession clear and hot, unfeigned. "Piss for him dude, piss for _me_..." Turning slightly as I nursed from his dick, he kissed Gary slowly and deeply, his piss still shooting hot and golden from that massive, glorious penis.

Gary broke the kiss and held his dick, pointing at me. I held Rob in my mouth, letting piss spurt and drool from the sides. A spurt, a dribble, then a dripping slow flow. Then _Piss_, and he began to participate in the obsession. Then a hot, full blast sailed into the melee and splashed onto me. Rob cheered.

"Yeah man that's it, give it to him! Let's see it man!" Rob blasted another full stream to me, then took his cock away. In a second, he was with me, on his knees before Gary, waiting. I put my wet arm up on his shoulder and held him beside me.

Gary smiled, then began to pour full force, spraying us both. Rob leaned forward and grabbed his semi-hard dick, and in a flash was drinking him, taking a big mouthful. Letting Gary's cock drop, he turned to me and spewed, shotgunned into my mouth, and kissed me in piss.

Piss, god it was hot, wild and beautiful! I sucked it from his mouth and swallowed, then I took the smaller man's hot organ and did likewise, taking a nice mouthful to share. Rob and I swapped it, then I took another. Before they could realize what I was doing, I pulled Gary down into a 3-way kiss and spewed piss for them both. His eyes closed and he slurped, gulping up what he could. We tongued in it; Rob was stroking Gary's cock and ready for more. But Gary pulled me up, wanting to complete the circle.

"Your turn! Give it to us man!" he said, and in a flash Rob was before me, waiting for my piss-load. I leaned onto Gary's muscled body and tried to relax. But I wasn't yet on the wavelength, and as I tried to relax a hot fart shot out behind me. Gary laughed uproariously; Rob wasn't pleased. But a few seconds later, I mumbled to them.

"OK man, OK... here ya go..." and began to open up. My piss was thick, hot and thick, strong and wild. Rob held my dick head lightly, his lips just behind my corona, as I pumped a nice slow stream of molten gold onto his tongue. He moaned low, his mouth full, but grunted and moaned his pleasure.

"Feed him buddy, yeah give it to him... oh man, let me have some too!" Gary said, and letting me stand alone he was on the floor beside his pal. I spurted hot streams into his face, onto his body, and then let him take the nectar. He gulped, swallowed, then took a mouthful as he'd seen us do. From above, I watched the two glorious studs swapping my piss, then offered them more so I could join in it.

Back and forth we went, sharing piss and kissing, pawing and probing one another's bodies. Our streams slowed, and mine ended. Gary said he had more, but would save it. I had as much in my belly as I'd had in my bladder. Morning coffee, the cocktail and now piss loading me, I'd have another full bladder in a short while. And they'd be ready to take it, too. But for now...

"Come on man, over here!" I said to Gary, and got him up onto a tarp on the long table. His legs up, his ass open, I reached beside us and found a tube of white machine grease. Industrial shit, the molybdenum and other materials in it were probably toxic, but we didn't worry about it. I slapped a gob on his hairy asshole and got into position. With a forceful slam, I buried my dick in his hard, hot body. He gasped, yelled in pain and pleasure.

"Fuck man, fucker! Goddam it, oh _fuck_!" He wanted me to stop, I know he did, but he wouldn't be a 'pussy' with his fuck-buddy present. He took it, and I slammed into him again, fully, probing his innards. A heavy hand stroked down my backside, and I was pushed forward, over Gary's supine body. My belly pressed onto his cock as my penis filled his asshole. Strong hands parted my legs, making me stand with my feet wide apart. I felt hot sloppy goo on my anus. I thought of Dean a fraction of a second before Rob pushed his fat, hard dickhead onto my asshole and then...

White lightening. He tore into me with a frenzy, ripping into my guts and sending shock and pain shooting through my body. The force was transferred through me and I slammed into Gary that much harder, and all three of us bellowed in the accomplishment of our Sodomitic embrace.

"Fucker! Goddam it, fucker!" "Yeah man, fuck me, harder!" "Take it man, yeah that's it open up, take it fucker, I'm in you man, fucker!"

"Fuck me man, yeah fuck me! Give it to me!" "Man open that asshole, spread it, yeah open up baby!" "Yeah fuck this hole man, show me what you got fucker! Gimme that _cock_!"

On we went, bucking in that hot three-way embrace. The smell of piss permeated us, filled the room as we fucked and kissed. Rob forced himself across my shoulder again to kiss Gary, I turned sideways to join them. My asshole was screaming, pain and hot agony forcing me into wilder thrusting within Gary's tight, welcoming hole. His body bucked under me, forcing me to pound his prostate as Rob's huge body pressed on us both. Rob began to groan, then yell an obscene torrent as he neared the end.

"Fuckin' ay man, yeah fucker, that's it here you go fucker I'm gonna shoot it I'm gonna CUM I'm gonna fuckin' CUM MAN I'M CUMMING! AGGGGH!" and his thrusts pounded into me. I felt his dick swell even more and he slammed up me with a powerful grip around my body, impaling me as his load burst inside me.

It sent me and I too began a yelling, cursing tirade as I went over the edge. Gary was shouting his encouragement as I held Rob's dick up my ass and poured my cum into the hot man beneath me.

"Aggh fuck yeah man, goddam it me too I'm cummin' man, I'm gonna shoot it here you go oh FUCK OH FUCK MAN I'M CUMMING TOO!"

Gary simply roared and yelled, growling and bucking like a wildman, spreading his ass wider to me as I dumped spurt after hot spurt of semen deep into him. Rob's hot cum flooded into my ass at the same time, leaking around his shaft as he could not hold himself buried up my tunnel in that strange three-way position. As our sperm shot, we all coupled and completed.

Gary humped and bucked, writhing on the table as we fucked him. It felt as though Rob's gargantuan cock drilled right through me and into his buddy's asshole. Gary joined us a few seconds later, yelling in non-verbal howls and grunts as his spunk shot up and across his chest, onto me as I mounted him. We came, shooting our manly essences together. My load was planted deep in the hot muscleman's body; my guts took the seed from the glorious giant behind me.

Funky and hot, gasping for air in the stuffy trailer, we finished unloading our heavy nuts and shared our spooge. I licked the sweat from Gary's forehead as Rob continued to stroke his huge reaming-tool in and out of my aching hole. We collapsed slowly, trying to catch our breath, as Gary's cock poured out the remainder of his piss.

It took minutes, but at last we had to break apart. Rob's cock hung sloppy and slick, gleaming with sperm. Gary's hole leaked a gob of semen, and I took it up on a finger. With a perverted smirk, they both leaned in and we slobbered and kissed in it together. It was time to go, and we dressed quickly.

Before Rob pulled those beautiful jeans back on, I'd yanked his spunky, funky jockstrap off.

"This is mine!" I said, claiming my trophy. He didn't protest as I put it on, and stuffed my other into my hip pocket.

The guys headed back out first, and I followed a minute later. I gave them the 'straight-guy nod' as I passed and went back up to the office, Gary rubbing his ass while Rob grinned...

———————

May became June and then drifted toward August... the hot summer was at its peak and so was the trucker and contractor rutting season, it seemed. I managed to fuck or get fucked at least once a week, enjoying the men and often having second and third meetings. George became quite a regular, expecting me to be his first lay whenever he arrived, which had been every Saturday night for most of the summer. He was worth it, but the sedate pace of his sexual action became boring. Still, it was always a satisfying fuck and that delicious dessert.

There were others too. It was not uncommon for me to take the walk about the facility on my shift and find one or more men discreetly waiting to see if I'd be out. Two of the regular construction men, friends of Juan's, became quite enamored of hot piss play. We'd slip into a trailer and I'd drain them. They weren't into man-fucking, only one of the guys even really liked getting sucked off. Whether they were straight, gay, married or what, I never knew. But *Piss*, the Obsession had gotten them and they couldn't resist pouring hot, funky, beautiful Piss from their hard cocks into a willing, thirsty throat.

I drank piss once or twice a week it seemed. Joe still dropped by the apartment once a month or so, but he'd found a woman who would play with him. Being truly straight, he preferred that, but he never forgot the hot fag-buddy who'd first showed him the joys of sharing Piss; nor did he forget the 'man-connection' of it which he intuitively understood and enjoyed. *Piss*, so hot, so satisfying! My jockstrap stayed on my body 24 hours a day and seven days a week it seemed, because I never knew when I'd get piss, and I didn't want to be without it when I was drinking a hot man's load. Jockstraps and Piss: my Obsessions.

Our truck-wash had gone up and was all but ready to go into operation.

The work was finished, we only had to fire it up, make sure everything operated the way intended, and the finishing touches on the concrete drives around it would complete the Back Forty. I thought it would be a fine addition, a nice new sandbox for my testosterone-charged jockstrap playground.

The building had 4 washing bays, huge and tall, and could fully clean a tractor and 53' trailer in 3 minutes. It was nice. There was a side room with water pressure and heating equipment, and a private restroom, open but not marked and hardly anyone would ever know it was there. Even the contractor and management, such as Mike, had all but forgotten about it.

We took a final tour of the new construction late on a fine Thursday afternoon: Mike Wales, terminal owner Joe Hillberg and myself, Don Schmidt the general contractor and a couple of his men. Gary and Rob were along, and a couple others. Gary was half in the bag, and twice made funny gestures behind Hillberg. I held a straight face easily enough, but I thought Mike was going to lose it. The guy *was* boring as hell...

The tour ended, and Mike took Joe and his buddies into the coffee-shop to congratulate themselves. Rob, Gary and a couple others lagged behind, then we all turned away from the troop going back to the building. They had a jug of mixed drink and some definite intent in their eyes.

"Hey man, this is Pete and Marty. They're good ole boys, we thought you might wanna get with us on this. We're gonna christen this place, break it in right!" Gary snickered, Pete was already hard in his Carhartt's. I smiled.

"Yeah? What you got in mind?" Marty groped at himself, his fat dick showing clearly in his faded, shredded jeans. His cock-head popped out a hole just below his left pocket. I grinned again.

"Well, why don't we all go in that back room and lock the door man, see what happens?" Gary suggested, Rob and the others mumbling assent.

"Yeah, come on, we'll have a great time."

We made an agreement to meet up at the door of the men's room at 7:00 that evening; the top brass would be gone, I had a key and we'd do just that. Go in together, lock the doors and let whatever might happen, happen.

All four of them were waiting when I walked around in the twilight, the tower flood lamps were installed, but that circuit was not yet powered up. An empty materials box lay beside the door. *Do Not Stack More Than 4 High*, it said. We laughed our asses off at that.

"Nope! Gonna be stacked FIVE high tonight!" one of the guys said. I opened the door, and we stepped in.

The room was fairly large, one stall with a toilet in the corner, a wide to-the-floor urinal beside that. A vanity and sink were opposite, and a small tidy shower stall behind the main stall. The whole was done in a fine tile, clean and ready. The door closed behind us and locked; there were no windows and I flipped on the overhead lights. I grinned at the men, and once more Marty was already beginning.

He had his jeans off in seconds, a fat hard dick standing up in a mass of reddish pubes. He jerked himself to his full 6" and patted Pete on the ass with the other hand. Gary was quick to get on his knees, pulling the front of Rob's jeans open, and slurping, sucking on that hot power-cock in hunger and need. I began to rip off my own clothing, and quickly stood among them with my full, dirty jockstrap poised for action.

My dick throbbed and thickened, and Pete stepped up to fondle me.

"Yeah dude, that's a nice pack you got there," and slowly leaned down to take it. Flopping my meat out the side of the pouch, he sucked and slurped, his jeans falling to his ankles. Marty was on his knees behind him, burying his face in Pete's hairy crack. The men began a low moaning, writhing and working one another.

My dick stood out fully, hot and slick, and Rob was ready to get down on that meat and get nasty. He grinned in horny need and was on his knees in front of me, quickly taking me to the hilt. Pete was beside him, and they swapped me back and forth, licking along my shaft and slurping each other's faces and tongues as they did. The groaning beside us became louder, and we realized that Marty had his cock buried in Gary's asshole, with Gary standing and holding onto the edge of the vanity. A tube of lube rested beside his hand, and I wasn't the only one who'd brought fresh poppers.

They bucked, worked it together and I moved away from the two slurping cocksuckers in front of me to take a place behind Marty. He thrust his short cock into Gary, reaching around to stroke and jack him, his thick furry legs leading up to his round, hairy buns. I pushed on his shoulders, hard, and forced him down and back. Grabbing the lube, I slicked up and parted his cheeks, then slammed into him with force.

He howled, yelled in pain and tried to work away. But as when Rob had fucked me while I was buried in Gary's asshole, Marty had nowhere to go and simply thrust into his bottom-boy harder. Gary yelled and pushed back, the three of us beginning a hot humping writhing fuck standing at the sink. I could see us in the mirror, looking at my own insanely gleaming eyes as their heads bobbed up and down. Gary's face lifted up, his eyes clenched shut in hot anguish, his cock leaking.

For a long moment I fucked into Marty's hole, then released him. He gasped slightly as I pulled free, then I turned and Rob was standing full height before me, grinning in heat.

"On your back Matt!" He commanded, and I lay down, handing him the lube as he got into position. Lifting my legs up high and wide, he greased his cock and then in powerful heat, thrust into me to his balls. My head reeled, my body screamed in wild mansex, and I yelled encouragements.

"Yeah fucker, goddam it! Fuck me man!" and the others began to join in. Poppers went from hand to hand, penises slammed into throats and assholes; we traded. Marty fucked me after Rob had ripped me open; it was hot and nice to feel his thick cock trying to probe me, but as one after another took turns entering and drilling, I wanted only to feel Rob's massive manhood slam into me again.

We got to that a bit later; but not until after all four of the guys' cocks had been in my ass, and I'd explored all of their assholes with my dick as well. I stood and thrust my cock forward, my jock sweaty, damp and soiled with the secretions of those four men. I let myself relax with a hit of poppers and while Rob fucked Marty on the floor, I opened up and began to piss on them.

The cheer went up, and within a second Gary had his lips around my corona, sucking and slurping my piss as it shot out hot and hard. He gulped, savored and swallowed, then, not being greedy, he took a large mouthful and spat it onto Pete's genitals, then began to lick and clean him.

Rob stood up, leaving Mart on his back, and joined me, standing beside me, his arm about my waist. Together we pissed and watered the men, shooting our streams on them, into faces and hair, onto dicks and arms, onto the walls. We slurped kisses and stroked each other's cocks. The fucking went on, switching positions, switching partners.

We shared piss, drinking and showering, flinging it around the room. One by one we blew our loads. Into each other's mouths, up our asses. Rob pumped his cum deep into me; I writhed and bucked and shot my load into Gary's mouth while Rob penetrated and fucked me. The other guys were 69'ing and rolling about on the tile, apparently they shot at virtually the same second. They both came up with gobs of semen dripping from their lips, then began to kiss.

Rob, Gary and I jumped into the fray and we shared it all 5 ways. Coated with piss and sweat, cum and spunk, we finally wound down. We left one by one, slipping away with kisses and back-slapping into the dark night of the Back Forty. The room had been initiated. But that was the beginning of the end for me at Hennepin Playground.

Mike Wales called me into his office the following week. He looked glum, and I knew it wasn't good. But in no way did I think he'd have the goods on us as he did. He began with mentioning the lot runners. There had not been an issue with them in quite some time, so as soon as he brought that up, I knew there was far more.

"Yeah, well Matt, you know how it is. We just cannot have the reputation that that kind of shit puts on us. Hell..." He paused, phrasing things carefully.

"You remember the fucking fist-fight we had in the restaurant, two homo truckers duking it out. One all pissed off because the other didn't fuck him hard enough or some stupid shit." He looked right at me. He knew the truth of that one; Doug had let him in on most of it.

That didn't bother him at all, and I knew it. He paused a long moment, then went on.

"But that's no big deal. There's more." I waited.

"Couple of the guys from Arapaho Construction got wild in the new building I heard. Got pretty crazy over there." I was looking down, I knew what was coming next.

"Yup, you guys broke it in real well. *Real* well." I said nothing. He continued.

"Of all the stupid reasons to have to shit-can you man, why that? Goddam it, I never thought it would be for fucking around with the workers for Christ's sake!"

He was distraught, genuinely let down. I felt shitty; I <u>felt</u> like a total let-down. But it was done.

"Man, you got 3 weeks' vacation pay coming, and you'll get it. But..." He paused once again. "You're off the schedule as of now." I nodded.

"Go back to school, Matt; get a fucking grip on yourself." He sat motionless, expressionless. I nodded again, then turned and slowly walked out of his office.

With that, Hennepin Transfer and Terminal was in the past.

GUYS FROM PURDUE
PURDON'T

With a few fast phone calls and some creative financing through my dad's bank, I'd made up my mind to move to Indiana. I'd been accepted into several Master's degree programs, but Indiana U was one of the best in the country for music studies. The courses I would be needing to start with were available at the secondary campus in Fort Wayne, which they shared with Purdue University. IUPU-FW, quite the mouthful.

I gave notice for the apartment, drove down to Ft. Wayne to scope out another place, and opted for a small 3rd floor townhouse-type apartment not far from campus. The granite Coliseum and the St. Mary's River formed two important landmarks. And, the city was convenient both to Chicago and to Indianapolis or even Detroit for recreation. I packed and moved down in the middle of August, carrying everything I needed in my moving-out present from Dad, an immaculate 1972 Coupe DeVille.

My trip was uneventful (even an over-night stop at the Maryland *en route* wasn't much to remember,) and I quickly got settled in to Apartment 301. I toured the campuses and found my way around. My phone was installed and I sent out cards with the new address info. I met my neighbors: mostly students, but a few married couples, families, and single men. Oh yeah, the guy directly below my unit on the first floor was a fine one. Almost certainly straight, nonetheless Jack had all the signs of the quintessential Horndog. I got the impression he'd go for anything or anyone who might get him to shoot his load.

I wasn't sure about a casual hook-up or fuck-buddy that close to my own home, especially a married one, but... if things lead us that way I wouldn't say no. I registered for my classes on a Thursday and stopped for burgers on the way back to the apartment. Cruising out Coliseum Boulevard, I spotted Jack walking along the road in the thick humidity of the day. I pulled over and waited for him.

"Goddam man, thanks!" he said. Sweat streaked down his face in the 99 degree, 99% humidity of Fort Wayne in August. His pits reeked, and his clothes were coated with shop dust, machine grease and automotive oils. A grease monkey, how cliché. How nice.

"Yeah buddy, way too hot to be stumbling all the way home. What's up with your car?" I knew he had one, a spiffy classic Mustang.

"Man, I wrench on it, but I got no license you know... DUI." Yeah, yeah, what a surprise huh?

"Bummer, well... can't promise anything, but I go up and down this way often you know. Maybe can work something out."

"Hell most times I don't mind, the walk is good. But just when I been busting ass like this, and then got to get home you know. All I want is something to drink. Got nothing at home but water though..." He let the idea trail off.

"Um, yeah... I suppose. Sucks, huh? Well, I'm sure I got a couple beers, maybe you'd like to...?" He jumped onto that idea before I could finish the invitation.

"Hell yeah man, damn! I'd fuckin' _love_ a beer. Hey, this Coupe is a nice old girl!" He stretched his hands out in front of the AC louver. I turned onto Coldwater and headed back to the complex. We chatted cars and engines, GM vs. Ford and the like. I swung into the parking lot.

Within a few seconds of parking, Jack was out and heading into our building. He was decently built, stocky even, with a thin, stubbly attempt at a goatee growing on his chin. The moustache wasn't bad; the 'beard' looked really sleazy, hot and wild. His sloppy shop cap was turned backwards on his head.

He held the security door open for me and I hauled my purchases from the bookstore up with us. He didn't bother to stop in his own place, but followed me to the 3rd floor. My place was clean, cool and sedate. The blinds were drawn.

"Aw man, yeah! Nice in here! My AC isn't working." I figured it was the electric bill that wasn't working, but said nothing. He glanced around, the pale couch concerned him.

"Hey go ahead man, it's OK."

"Nah man, I'm all sloppy, I don't wanna sit on that. I'll get grease on it," he said. "I oughtta go change..." It was obvious he didn't want to leave the cool room, _or_ pass up his beer.

"Man, don't worry about it, I'm gonna go kick this stuff off. I'm not all that clean either you know." What a vapid suggestion; but it actually worked!

"Hum, maybe I should just take my jeans off too?" He plopped down on the entry doormat and began untying his boots even before I could respond. I nodded and grinned.

"Sure! Totally cool!" I calmly got us a beer while he took his clothes off.

His body was a bit pudgy, thick belly and what could have been a nice chest. His man-tits were just slightly too big though, and it probably wouldn't get any better with time. But he wasn't bad, by any means. He peeled his jeans off and the pouch of his white Jockey's sagged under the weight of some substantial meat. Jack's chest-hair was like unto his beard, scraggly and unimpressive. But what was there was pasted down to his body with perspiration, and was not unappealing.

I looked him over thoroughly, not even bothering to try to be discreet. The guy just stopped into my apartment for the first time, and within 90 seconds had stripped to his shorts! I wasn't _not_ going to check him out. I gave him a cold can of beer and went to the bedroom. Kicking out of my shoes, I undid my belt, and let my own jeans drop off. I was bending over to gather things up when I heard Jack behind me.

"Um yeah man, this hits the spot! Dang..." He gulped from his beer can, standing in the door of my bedroom. I stood up and looked him up and down. His cock was plump, if it was hardening I couldn't tell, but there was surely plenty of it in any case.

"Yeah good! Good man! I didn't bring mine though." I stood shameless in my sweaty jockstrap, the bulge full and thick.

He held up a can for me.

"I brought it back here man, knew you'd be needing it too." He took a tentative step into the bedroom. I reached for the beer, cracked it open and took a swig myself.

The bed ran sideways to the doorway, and my nightstand and small chair were between the bed and the outside wall. I flipped on the TV as I went around the foot of the bed. I got to the far side, Jack still just inside the door. I tossed my clothing on the chair and set my beercan on the bedside table. I swung myself onto the bed, sitting up with my back at the pillows. My legs stretched down, my basket thrust upward. Jack checked me over and took another step forward.

"Um, yeah, man... thanks for the beer. Really hits the spot you know..." He was looking carefully up and down my body. "Nice and cool back in here man. Yeah, nice..."

"Yeah man, glad to give ya one. No problem, you need to cool off, I know... get all hot and sweaty at work you gotta kick back." I smiled at him. He grinned back.

"For sure bro, no shit, thanks! Really do need to kick back, chill out. Get so *hot* you know... all day in that shop. You know?"

"Hey bud, kick back. Hop up here and let's have a beer you know?" I patted the ample area beside me on the bed.

Jack looked a bit hesitant, but he wanted it. He stepped once more and paused, then walked up to his side and got onto the bed, stretching out beside me. His hot basket was definitely thickening, the curve of his cock now distinct in the clinging fabric.

"Hot man, you look nice. Like to kick back with a buddy you know? Just two dudes chillin' out..." he said. I nodded and smiled nicely.

"You bet. We can handle that man, for sure. Help you get real relaxed you know, take a load off..." He grinned widely now.

"Man I got a load on me too, big load..." His hand slid to the front of his jockeys; I watched him indicate the way. Sliding my hand across the coverlet to him, I reached up and began to fondle him. He laid back and half closed his eyes, letting me slide a finger into the pouch opening. His own hand moved to stroke and paw at my jockstrap. He looked down, surprised at the hardness and readiness of my body under his touch.

"Man, let's get these last things out of the way! Let me get those shorts off you and see what you got there, huh?" I suggested. He slipped his briefs down, and his long slim cock flopped over, hot and beginning to lengthen noticeably. He had to be over 8" but maybe 5" around, if that. I wrapped my hand around his shaft and stroked slowly up and down.

"You like to get your cock sucked man?" I said softly, non-threateningly.

"Fuck yeah man, you like to suck dick? So do I sometimes... yeah man, let's!"

Within a few seconds we were positioned and holding one another in a wild 69. He liked to straddle atop me and jam his dick into my throat, and slam his own face deeply onto my thick rod. We slurped and sucked, grinding and stroking at one another. I slid my finger into his ass crack and stroked up and down the line. He squirmed back, trying to move away.

"Aw man, naw, I'm not... I mean, you can't... um... I don't wanna fuck or anything. Can't we just suck dick? I'm not into men's asses you know..."

I calmed him quickly.

"Hey dude, sure! No, it's cool! I'm into most anything you know... I like it all. Like to suck cock, fuck, get sucked and fucked. Hell I like to get in the shower and piss on each other." His face perked up, piqued.

"No shit? Wow, that would be fun!" Again, it was just too easy...

I suggested we play around, have a couple more beers and we could experiment a little bit. Get ourselves stoked up, hot and full, then go piss and play. He liked the idea. Still pawing and playing, sucking and stroking our hot hard dicks, we lay on the bed and drank beer, letting the mindless TV play on the dresser, all but ignored. After maybe half an hour, he was squirming a bit.

"Hey dude, you ready? Man I'm not sure how much longer I can hold this." I agreed. I'd not drained since hours earlier; I'd been holding back way too long, not wanting to piss until Jack was ready to join me. We got up and went into the small bathroom.

I'd put small, low-wattage gold chandelier bulbs in the fixtures. The result was a kind of faint, flickering candle-light. It was seductive and intimate; lighted but private, secure. I closed the door and turned on the hot shower. In moments the golden glow was also thick with steam. Jack loved it.

We stepped into the shower and closed the frosted sliding door. I stroked Jack's body, fondling his belly, his ample man-breasts, his hot prong cock. I got on my knees to suck him and he was agitated, worried. As so often with newbies, his prejudice and programming made him uncomfortable, worried, even though he knew the intention getting in there was to share some piss.

"Man," he whispered. "I really gotta go, stop sucking me or I won't be able to hold it man... c'mon, I'm gonna piss..."

Not reacting to his caution, I cupped his balls and sucked nice and slowly, firmly on his cock head. I held him tightly in my lips, and ran my strong hands up the inside of his legs. I rubbed his belly, then pressed lightly as I suckled and pulled. I took about half his long, slim dick onto my tongue and silently encouraged him to let go... let go. He couldn't hold back any longer.

"Aw man, aw... man, I can't hold it!" and a firm, full stream began to flow into my mouth. Hot *piss*...

I gathered up a good mouthful, then pulled back. The wonder and amazement on Jack's face was precious; he loved the idea, the whole concept. His obsession with piss had begun long before this moment, but obviously he'd never been able to put anything into practice. He watched in horny fascination as I held his spunky piss in my mouth, then spat the whole load onto his cock and balls. He loved it.

Holding his cock at the base, I controlled his flow and I'm sure the back-pressure in his urethra and bladder also added to the sensations. He ground towards me, offering me to suck again on his cock as I gripped him. I slurped at the slit, tasting and licking.

"Oh man, dude, that's hot; take it man OK? Take it..." He leaned back a bit, letting his manly stuff hang hot and free. I pulled his corona into my lips and released the grip on his tube. Once more his piss flowed, full and unabated. I knelt in my jock, hot and steamy, and slurped more from him.

Filling my mouth again, I tilted my head back and let him dribble onto my chest. My mouth was open, and slowly, dramatically I _gargled_ that hot piss. He went crazy, loving it. Grabbing his dick at the base, he pointed at me, onto my body, into my face and spurted more. He flung his cock back and forth and sprayed the shower stall and both of us in his nectar. I gulped, then pulled him close for another nice drink.

"Man, damn... fuck that's hot!" He was ready for more, and I rose to my feet. Standing close, all but pressed up to him, I held my own penis and his hand tentatively reached to stroke me. I relaxed and let my full bladder rush and gush, a thick stream poured out, down his leg and onto his feet, his genitals, around us both.

"Mmmmm fuck yeah man, yeah, do it!" he whispered, watching in fascination, frightened at the thoughts he had going through his mind which had risen without any suggestion from me. I stopped the flow, and waited for him to decide. He paused, began to bend his knees, then straightened up again.

"You wanna try it, don't you?" I asked softly, but he didn't react, staring at my cock while he gently held me.

"There's nothing bad or filthy about it you know, it's hot and salty, fine... It's not like fucking or any of that stuff." I used the example of what I knew he did not want. He smiled, and with no further trepidation Jack knelt, taking my dick into his mouth.

As I had done, he ran his hand up my thigh, cupping my balls. The other pressed on my belly, on my bladder, encouraging me to relax, to release. I let him hold my dickhead in his lips, waiting in that fine anticipation, and opened my tube for him.

Piss. He was receiving his first delicious piss.

Jack's eyes closed, his mouth savoring the delicate, velvetty texture, the salty goodness. With a supreme act of will, he took the mouthful he'd collected and gulped, swallowed it down. Then again. Then he began a low moaning, *groaning* in pure homo-sexual union and joy, my cock in his mouth. I pissed for him and he took it, sucking and gulping as fast as I could pour my hot gold.

With hands lifted up, raised and stroking my belly, he worshipped and received piss as an orante, a suppliant. In long hot moments of pure piss-joy, he let himself float in total horny abandon. He drank me, a brand-new piss-drinker.

I slowed, stroked the side of his face, and he spit a mouthful of piss onto me. My cock and balls, my jock dripped the savory liquid, and he rose. His long, slim cock pointed upwards, rock hard and wet. He stroked himself and motioned to me.

"Man, I'm so hard now... take it ok? Get me off!" I got back on my knees, sucking him fast and hard. He thrust to the back of my throat, pushing between my tonsils, gagging me without trying. His slim cock hit my reflex as a fat, thick dick would not, but I held it and sucked him harder, deeper. He thrust and parried, bucked and then that hot groan began deep in his throat.

"Ugggh, man yeah... here it is dude, yeah man, I'm gonna SHOOT!"

His slit flared and with thick hot bursts the cum pumped deep into my ready mouth. Hot sperm gobbed up around his cockhead, my throat was too pegged to swallow it and I had to wait until he'd finished his orgasm before I could slurp it down. Hot seconds ticked by as he pumped and oozed.

At last he drew back, looking at me kneeling, my mouth stuffed with his load.

"Man, wow... yeah man that's what I needed..." Once more, dramatically I leaned my head back and gulped, swallowed his sperm He smiled.

"Aw dude, _yeah_! Fuckin' ay!"

I rose from the floor of the stall, and he was slopping the hot water over himself, rinsing quickly. He was done; my own hard cock was ignored.

"Yeah man, that's what I needed. Really hot stuff but I gotta get goin' you know my wife's goin' be getting supper ready and I gotta get back to see about them burner pans she's been griping about and yeah buddy that was HOT really needed a good cold beer, that hit the spot but better get moving here you know, been fun maybe we can watch the game this weekend or sumpin you think?"

I let him hop from the stall and towel himself off. By the time I got halfway caught up and had a towel around myself, Jack had gathered up his stuff and was dressed. He gulped the last of his beer in a flash, and while still babbling his run-on sentence about how much he had to leave, he let himself out. I shook my head, locked the door and went back into the hot steamy water. I'd take care of myself, and jack off while remembering his pissing, his newfound obsession. I wondered how it would play out for him, 'married' farm-boy and all?

I never found out. After that encounter, Jack studiously avoided any contact with me. Only once more I picked him up walking along Coliseum, on a brutally cold day in December. That day he wanted no part of any action with me though, and that was the last time I ever spoke to him.

The fall classes began and I had registered for a full set of grad courses.

Through the first 9 weeks or so, there simply wasn't time to screw around, as I was becoming accustomed to the routine. The level of scholarship demanded in my sessions was much higher than U-Minn undergrad. Even the topmost courses I'd had there paled in comparison.

I pushed along, and finished my first year of Master's studies. A summer job in Fort Wayne at the library of a religious graduate school nearby kept me going. I found my playmates here and there. There were undergrad athletes, so an occasional jockstrapper was do-able, but I hardly ever got to indulge my obsession for piss.

There was a disco bar on the edge of the downtown area, 'Up The Street.' Leather was OK and welcome on Saturday night, but by no means common. I had a recurrent hook-up three weekends running with a Fort Wayne motorcycle patrolman. He was a hunk, hot and horny, but amazingly vapid and immature for a professional supposedly 6 years older than me. Playing cops-n-robbers. That's not unusual I've since learned, but he was my first real enlightenment about it.

He was another 'Tim;' I hadn't yet formulated my Theory of Names, but it suited him. Tim liked to get fucked and get sweaty, but wasn't at all interested in shower play. It seemed nobody was. Piss was a real rarity; I was thirsty a lot. But Tim would buck and hump, and lift his rump most willingly to accept deep hot pounding, slamming ass-fucking and all the sperm I could pump into him. He left me a pair of really beautifully scented Jockey shorts and a T-shirt, a cop belt and a well-worn pair of knee-high motorcop boots. And of course I confiscated one of his wonderfully worn jocks...

The year flew by, events just a blur of scholarship, playing piano and viola, rehearsing and the rare but unremarkable couplings with a newfound buddy. In all cases though, those men turned out to be married, closeted, or just passing through.

My second year began, and I had big plans to wrap up my Master's degree. The first major assignment I had was for a course in contemporary composition. I undertook a survey of musical development in the works of Leonard Bernstein.

That meant charting virtually everything he'd published since 1945 note by note and chord by chord. While I focused on his Symphonies, the 3rd having just been printed in a study-sized score, I had to find scores for his most important musicals, his opera, smaller works and his mighty "*Mass.*" By the time I'd gotten my analyses into a manageable form, it ran to 120-some pages and I had to pay to have it typed up. Another music-student's cunt wife did it, at $1.15 a page, and then...

She had 'corrected' my work, making substantial changes in the second-to-last chapter. She'd basically removed and re-written all the information that supported my conclusions. I was livid.

"Why the hell would you just decide to re-write someone's paper like that?" I asked her.

"Well, I didn't want you to get into *trouble* with it you know. I *read* Larry's book about Bernstein; this is what you *meant* to say." She smiled, smug and cutsie-cute. She damn near got her face busted.

"Um, well, I'm sorry to have to tell you this, I didn't think I needed to. But..." I took a nice slow breath. "I didn't hire you to edit my work. Not so much as how I spell a name. I don't make spelling mistakes, ever. Maybe a typo; yes, that's why I wanted you to *type* it. Now then..." (another good caesura) "You're going to retype that paper, and do it exactly as I wrote it, or you're not getting paid. Is that clear enough for you, *Debbie*?" I spat her name out like it was filthy.

She was furious, saying I owed her $140.30 and she was going to send her husband after me. I once more wrote my phone number down for her, suggesting he call me immediately, and stormed out. I was going through another major piece of work when he called that afternoon. He apologized profusely, and insisted she would redo the thing. It amounted to retyping perhaps 40 of the sheets; he promised he would oversee it.

I agreed.

He arrived at my door with the paper the next day, and quite a sight he was. Twenty-six or so, finely built and killer blue eyes, Larry was a voice major (tenor) studying opera. He had one of those movie-star chins and a nice 'stache on smooth, silken skin. His jeans snuggled beautifully curved equipment. He smiled and I invited him in. He showed me the typed copy, the fucked-up copy and my manuscript. He said he'd gone over it from end to end himself; it was as I'd written.

Thanking him, I offered a drink. He accepted a cola, and we sat at my kitchenette to talk a bit. His darting eyes, nervous body-language and his pronunciation definitely indicated needs far beyond those which that castrating bitch Debbie could ever satisfy. Within a couple minutes, I had him up against the wall, my body mashed on his and our tongues tangling in hot kissing.

I ground my pelvis against him, our cocks hard and throbbing in our jeans. He loved it, moaning, grunting, groping and pawing me as I pawed him, but suddenly he pushed me back, away.

"Oh god, goddam it man, no! No! I can't do this man, no way! Shit..." He wiped his mouth on the back of his sleeve. "Shit man, I ain't no homo!"

I mumbled apologies, "Oh no man, I'm sorry, I didn't mean you were. It's just, well... you're a fine dude and no, *I'm* the homo. Sorry..."

He accepted that and left quickly. I figured he'd have to bury his face in Debbie's thick tits or her nasty gash as soon as he got home to prove to himself that he didn't want my kisses, didn't want my cock. And maybe that would even work, who knew?

I felt sorry for Larry; no, he wasn't a *homo*, not in the sense I understand it. He had never, ever found his likeness, that hot man *the same* as him. And in all likelihood, he never would. Sad. Even if he overcame the reticence on just the physical, sexual level, (and he desperately needed at least that,) he'd never manage to make the huge, intense and even spiritual leap to embrace his obsessions. To play on them, to explore his needs and wants, his impulses and desires, to orchestrate and harmonize the endless variations on those obsessions and channel them into something real, constructive. To harness the Obsession into self-awareness and to finally learn why and how his need and desire for someone *the same*, far from being strange or evil, would be his completion. His salvation. I held little hope for him.

The winter progressed; I earned top marks in my classes, but the lack of real stimuli and creative impulse had me at odds. I'd not heard from Tim LaRoque since our Chicago trip over a year before, and I'd just gotten a postcard from him. I called. He was thrilled to hear from me and we made tentative plans for the week after New Year's.

I had several important projects going when school closed down for the holidays, so I wasn't able to leave Fort Wayne. I wasn't going to be able to spend the holidays with my family. It was different, but not such a loss, we'd been mostly scattered for some time. Still, I wasn't sure what I'd do.

Christmas Eve found me pensive, a bit depressed as the holidays often do to people. I'd slept almost the whole of the 23rd, and this afternoon I was determined to go find some society, some interaction. Not really knowing anything but the disco in Fort Wayne, I was struck with a thought and called the gay crisis line.

No, I told the volunteer, it's not an emergency, not a crisis. I'm just feeling lonely and crappy and want to go out. Where's a decent bar to visit? Darren D spoke with me, apparently there was another Darren as well, Darren T. "D" was bubbly, effervescent, and wanted to talk anyhow.

"Well *shit* girl!" (Fuck, did we have Tim LaRoque on here again? Hehehe, too much!) "Of *course* that's a crisis! Anything that makes you feel down and out and shitty at *Christmas* is a crisis. Now then, what are you *into*? *Hmmm*?" She wanted to hear juicy tidbits and my hot ideas of this and that, you could tell.

"Well... just the usual really. I mean, I'm gonna get leathered up and go step out for the evening that's all. I'm not looking for anything heavy; I don't really need the bondage or S&M and w/s tonight you know?"

He sucked in his breath, the perverse little hiss meant he took the bait. "Oh my!"

"You know, if you want to go *play* and *really* enjoy yourself, you should go on down to Indy. That's a much nicer gay scene you know. They've got the Talon and the BodyWorks and the Ruby and you'd really, *really* like the PumpHouse. That's kind of a biker bar; the leather boys go there. In fact," I could hear the sheets of paper rattling, crunching and sliding around as he sifted through the various regional hand-outs and flyers, "They're having a Christmas Party tonight. Starts at 9:00. You can easily get ready and make it down there."

"Um, isn't that about a four-hour drive?"

"Oh god *no*, girl! Only like 120 miles, not bad at all. I used to go *all* the time when I had a car, well, you know that was before I met *Rob* so it's not important but..." He paused, choosing his words carefully. "If you *do* decide to go to the PumpHouse, you'll find black hankies and *yellow flags* all over the place honey, *all over*."

He'd convinced me, and gave me quick directions over the phone. But I wanted to talk a bit more, just to chat and tease the little queen.

"Isn't there anything going on in Fort Wayne tonight though? You'd think with three major universities and all, plus the regular guys, there would be some action tonight..." He asked me about school. I mentioned being enrolled with Indiana U, but at the IUPU-FW center.

"Oh god _no_ honey! Not students! They're _so_ fuckin' closeted it isn't funny. Maybe in Arts at IU but... the guys from Purdue Purdon't. They just _Purdon't_, so purdon't bother. Ain't _worth_ it!" I got a laugh out of it, and gave him a very quick account of Jack and Larry, the str8 boys.

"Oh god yes, Fort Wayne is _full_ of those poor boys, it's fuckin' _sad!_ These goddam hot, _HOT_ farm boys and they need _dick_ so bad it's just enough to make you _scream_ and here he is with this goddam corn-fed Indiana _cow_ of a wife! It's not _fair_ girl, I'm telling you, it's just not _fair_!"

I laughed and heartily agreed, then assured him I'd be going to PumpHouse. He wanted me to call back, Christmas Day would be fairly busy on the teen line, but he'd be at this number and please, let him know how it had gone. Please?

I said sure (yeah right) and got myself in focus for Christmas Eve at a leather bar. There were quite a few things to do, not just getting dressed and packing a grip for later. I didn't think a traffic stop somewhere between Marion and Allen Counties by an Indiana state trooper would be all that festive were I to be dripping leather and hardware. I had a good stash of cash from my parent's Christmas gift, so I opted on packing a full over-nighter and getting a motel-room as soon as I got to Indianapolis.

Within an hour, I was heading out, listening to an 8-track tape of Mahalia Jackson Christmas classics. I got out of the funk, and swapped Mahalia out for The Village People. I decided to stop for supplies, and got a snack for the road, some stuff for the room, and a case of beer. Then onto the freeway and south, heading to Indy for Christmas.

CHRISTMAS AT THE HOLIDAY INN

I decided Shell Oil needed to show a profit that quarter, and burned up half a tank of premium hauling ass to Indianapolis. I was driving into the city center just before sundown, and cruised around a bit to familiarize myself with the location. I found the PumpHouse, went past the BodyWorks and the Rainbow; then decided I'd better find a motel before it was too late. I'd called ahead to a couple samples, there seemed to be plenty of vacancies.

The motel closest to the PumpHouse was a total shit-hole, obviously the local by-the-hour dump. A black street thug motioned to me as I drove through the parking lot, trying to make a sale. I went around a corner and 2 blocks farther, and a rather new Holiday Inn rose 3 stories on my right. Perfect. I checked in, and was assigned an upper room, way around the back wing of the buildings on the second floor, number 238. There were quite a number of patrons about, folks getting ready for their family events the following day, traveling businessmen and so on. It was a nice place.

The room reminded me of Dwayne Hoover's motel-room. He'd checked into a Holiday Inn during a moment of psychotic instability and confusion, not realizing he in fact <u>owned</u> the property. "*Dwayne loved his room,*" Mr. Vonnegut wrote. "*It was so <u>neutral</u>!*" And so was this. A garish, multi-colored hotel bedspread, dark carpet to hide the nasties, a tasteless sofa-sized 'oil' painting, lots of nice clean tile and plenty of hot water. It was exactly what I wanted. The 'walnut-grained' desk-vanity-dresser-TV-stand-table had only 3 or 4 cigarette burns; not bad. The TV worked, and even had a remote control.

I laid out my canvas suit-bag, one of those fold-over things, and my small grip. My leather gear and a couple changes of clothes in the one, my shaving and fucking supplies in the other. I settled in, arranged my stuff and decided I'd just walk across the street to the hamburger joint for a quick supper, then get got-up in my leather. I took my time, enjoyed my burger and flirted with a couple of married guys.

One was quite fine; maybe 30-32 or so, with a scruffy beard and great body, just your basic Indiana workin' stiff and good ole boy. His wifelet was a nasty, chunky thing with that pasty skin and huge ass so common in the corn country; and she spotted my glances at her man right quickly. If looks could kill, the ashes of my wretched self would probably still be smoldering on the hard plastic bench in that goddam burger joint. She leaned over to him and I could hear her muttering.

"That sumbitch must be some kind'a _homo_ or fag or something! Don't you look back at him! Damn, he's staring at us!" Possibly he said something like, Well maybe you oughtta quit staring at _him_... She said more, but I ignored them at that point. He didn't meet my gaze, no doubt resigned to the wretched fate he himself had agreed to in those decisive words, "I Do." What amazed and saddened me was how many of those men would've chosen the other side of the mattress if they'd only known, known and really believed that they _could_. Fucking sad.

But in any case, I ate my snack, took a minute with a newspaper and then walked back to the hotel to dress. It was fully dark, and I intended to be at the Pump by 8:30 or so. The covercharge went from $2 to $5 at 9:00 PM. Entering my room I was again struck by the universal nature of motel rooms from one end of the country to the other. I could've been in Bangor, Maine, or Daytona Beach or Carlsbad, California as easily as Indianapolis. I loved my room; it was so _neutral_! But I was hopeful that the events of the night might be such to change, charge that neutrality with a positive burst of primal, sexual and *homo*-sexual energy.

I turned on the tube, letting some inane Hoosier with a really bad toupee read the Christmas Eve weather to me, complete with the Carol of the Bells in the background and all that happy crap. I laid out the gear and accessories I was planning to wear, then sat on the edge of the bed and picked up the phone.

I made a quick call up to Crookston, wishing my family the best for the day and talking to all in turn. My mother was a bit miffed that once again I'd taken off into parts unknown for purposes unfathomable, but we were all happy to exchange our greetings. I was a bit wistful as I rang off, but as much as I'd had to come to terms with my own nature, my sexuality and my obsession, so I'd long since reconciled with my family.

Turning back to the bed, I began to dress for the night. Once more I was all but torn in trying to select which jockstrap I wanted to wear. I'd brought along 2 favorites which I'd seasoned and broken in by swimming, running and playing hockey. Of course I had Dean's fabulous blue jock, still unwashed after all the hot fucking, sucking and pissing I'd done in it, beginning on and with him. I had one from Danny Meinrad; one from Bill Macey as well as the yellow one he'd given me, and 3 others I'd taken from various truckers and construction men during my tenure at the Hennepin Terminal, and also several new ones. Ah, decisions, decisions...

Arranging the eleven I'd brought with me on the bed, I compared, evaluated, rationalized. The Blue... ummm, always my favorite. The spunky, funky white ones, each one with its own hot memories attached. Red and black were new, the black hadn't even been worn yet. I looked at the oldest 'favorite,' a once-upon-a-time-white Duke supporter, the pouch fraying and soft, the two ass-straps smeared and discolored from fucking. The brown stains weren't exactly glamorous, but a little rectal residue with all that lube, sweat, piss and semen just came with the territory.

Dean's blue jock reminded me (as always) of the Chicago trip, and I wished I'd asked that hot hunk Nick Stoddard if he'd had a jockstrap, or perhaps had one of his late brother's. But I hadn't; so, finally I opted for that old Duke. I'd sucked str8 athletes in it, taken Kent in it, fucked guys in it, and it had been the one I was wearing that fateful night when Dean Cordell raped me and forced me to drink piss, forced me to drink *his piss* the very first time. *This* jockstrap was the 'Theme' to my Obsessions; I slid it on.

Once I had it strapped, wrapped around my loins and my fine manly equipment, I gently, lovingly lifted the beautiful blue Bike, crusty and stiff with the residue of many fuckings, of hot sucking, of piss and just plain sweaty wearing... and the residue of my night in Purgatory, the Piss Party that lead to my Resurrection. I sniffed it, licked it and chewed on it for a moment. Dean... oh god; Dean, what did you do to me?

I laughed softly, remembering that night in the trough. I'd embraced my Obsession in all its variations, sought to create and compose new variations. New variations which might surpass others in shades of nuance, but certainly not intensity or volume. Nothing would surpass the Delta Tau house, nor did I want it to... ever.

I began to dress, pulling on the faded soft Levi 501's Nick Stoddard had given me. A red strappy T-shirt and red-checked flannel lumberjack shirt went atop, thick white boot socks on my feet. I slid on a wide, plain black leather belt and tucked my flags in the back left pocket. Navy blue, grey, yellow... I slid my chaps around myself, and zipped up the sides. Then I pulled on Tim the Motorcop's Dehner boots, and cinched the small buckle straps just below my knees.

A biker wallet on a chain and keys on a clip completed my gear. I stepped to check it out, glancing into the mirror from several angles. Not bad, I decided, not bad... I had riding gloves and a biker hat ready, then made sure the lining was securely zipped into my jacket. I was prepared for the evening, come what may.

As I exited my motel room, several other guests noticed the wild apparition in black leather locking the door and heading into the parking lot. One lone man stood at his window, unself-consciously watching closely. His longing was transparent, and I could only assume he was yet another married Hoosier so badly needing to find his like, someone *homo-* to himself. Settling into my car, I was quickly on the way out of the parking lot and up to the PumpHouse.

Traffic was very sparse, most people having arrived at their homes, their parties, their motels by that hour. A cold-looking rent-a-cop stood at the driveway of the PumpHouse lot, and when I signaled my turn he directed me into the half empty (half full?) parking area. I chose a spot near the far corner, easily accessible to the other gate. Hopefully they would open it as the party broke up.

The entryway was long, opening from a corner door. A gaggle of 5 or 6 men stood beside the inner door, checking out the patrons. The seated doorman asked for the full $5 cover-charge, making me a bit irritated. Then, checking me up and down, he requested to see my ID. Tugging my wallet from my back pocket, I fished out a bill and my license, knocking my student ID out in the process.

"Oh, you're a student?" he lisped, his voice belied the hairy chest and full leather gear. He smiled, his eyes golden, matching the brass band around his right biceps.

I grunted, "Yup... IU -- Fort Wayne."

"Well then, no cover for you. Chicken and wrinkles get in free!" He thought himself quite funny. Actually, I liked him, but had the idea I wouldn't want this leather-queen all pissed off at me. Chicken huh? I'd been taken into bars without drinking since age 14, and gay bars since 15, and had never before been called 'chicken,' ever. Oh well, so what? Merry fuckin' Christmas.

I said so too, laughing, "Merry fuckin' Christmas, Brad!" noting the nameplate on his vest. He grinned and introduced me to Daddy Mike.

Mike thought the seasonal greeting was a scream, and gripped my hand tightly. There were 3 Daddys at the door, with Brad and 2 other Boys. Once within, more than half the clientele were in full leather regalia, chaps, jeans, boots... Body harnesses that took my breath away. The Cellblock in Chicago had a leather emporium, and I'd seen a body harness on a mannequin, but never on a muscled, greased up leatherboy. He was hot, the front strap leading into a leather G-string pouch that was amply filled. Even allowing for the character of leather and the shape of the strap augmenting his masculine curves, there was no doubt that the contents of that pouch were fine indeed.

I got to the service-well and bought a beer. I walked around the half-filled room. The bar formed a corner, set along the 2 sides of the back walls. The center of the room was a hardwood dance floor, corralled much like the one at Alfie's. As with my motel-room, there was something familiar yet generic about it. Alfie's, LoadingZone, Cellblock, Atlanta Eagle, the Detroit Interchange... The Corral in Denver... it could have been any of them, all of them. I was at home in a second.

Smoke curled up and around from several cigars and many cigarettes. Daddys and Boys, leather queens and a couple of genuine hard-core biker types moved about, smiling and talking, pawing one another nicely. They kissed, danced, sat and hugged. Several older men, the wrinkle contingent in their polyester slacks and dress shirts, ogled all and sundry. At the far end of the bar sat a man easily in his late seventies, if not older. He grinned at me and motioned, waving me over to himself.

"Well hey there stranger! I haven't seen you in here before! I'm Ronny." He extended a hand. "Where you from?"

"Down from the Fort tonight, didn't want to stay up at school alone on Christmas Eve," I said. "Matt," and took his large, strong hand. I was impressed.

Another elderly man came up as we were doing the introductions. "Geez RON-da," he gushed. "How'd you get ahold-a THIS hot MAN already?" The feminine shit; I guess it just goes on and on, huh? Fuck it.

Ronny bought me a drink and we talked a good bit. He had stories of the 'old days,' and he meant olden days. An actual working cowboy born in the Montana *Territory*, he'd traveled the country and done it all. He'd been in the Army at age 15, well before the Second World War. In fact, he'd enlisted well before the First World War, the Great War. He shared his birthday with President Lincoln, the one impending six weeks hence would be his ninety-second.

The gay-rights movement of the 1970's was all strange and new to Ronny, he wasn't at all sure how he felt about it. "In our day, nobody said boo shit about any of that," he told me. "Out on the range, who else were you gonna fuck but your bunkmate? And he's gonna fuck you... hell, the ride-master knew it, and paired guys up with that in mind. And soldiers been fuckin' one another since the Punic Wars, ain't nobody gonna pretend otherwise."

But he was fun to talk to, a realist and a very insightful man. Many other patrons came up to pay court, pay their respects, before going on with the events of the evening. I spent a good half hour or more with him, then pried myself away to cruise the room. The crowd had grown considerably, and I wanted to see more of the hot leathermen and boys, see who else might want to dance, drink, sing a carol or two, then go back to someone's motel room and get nasty.

We had the Jingle Bell Rock, then Elvis, more. Rather eclectic selection from the DJ, and men moved with the music. I felt a tug at my elbow and a plump, bald guy was grinning and asking me to dance. His vest hung open, revealing the hairless, pale mounds of his body. Large, non-descript tattoos heavy on the blue ink were smeared across his upper arms.

"Come on, let's loosen up!" His smile and genuine good nature were almost infectious. I had to smile back, and shrugged to the 3 guys I'd been standing amongst. I'd not actually been involved in their conversation, but while I stood at the rail along the wall, they'd turned to open their circle, silently including me should I care to talk. They grinned and nodded, one gave me a thumbs-up.

"Well hell, ok... I'm Matt."

"Jerome!" He was shorter than me, perhaps five-foot-ten. He wasn't hugely obese, but sure had a good 30 or 40 pounds he could've done without. He pushed into the crowd on the dance floor, selecting an area in the middle of it all.

We began to wiggle and swing, neither of us quite sure what the latest disco 'step' might really be. It was doubtful anyone else had paid attention either; but all were enjoying the sounds and moves, their proximity to other horny, sweating men in leather. All alike, all *homo*-... it was fine, seductive and rich. I pondered the sameness in all its variance; or the almost infinite individuality created from the one paradigm.

The narrow palette from which the scene had been painted nonetheless showed a scope far beyond expectations. Black leather and faded denim, denim and leather and flannel and some leather with denim; then the glint of a chromed chain or badge, an armband and a flash of a bandanna, blue or red, yellow and pink and purple and green...

The generic nature of the PumpHouse was readily apparent in the patrons. The faces of a strange couple reminded me of Holden and Halsted; a leather-daddy and his boy were complete ringers for Warren and Carl. Three or four of the lone-wolves could have been the illustrious Marky J, his image the quintessential look for leathermen from one end of the world to the other. Variations on a theme, they played variations on their own fetishes, their own obsessions.

Tight jeans and rounded-toe boots; chaps and vests; leather biker jeans and knee high boots; flannel shirts *sans* sleeves. Toned bodies and muscles, body hair and beards, moustaches, the air itself charged with testosterone, masculinity at its zenith. Jerome looked about, enjoying being part of the whole, being wrapped up in the scene. Among the striking characters of this and every leather bar, there had to be a couple of trolls too; as usual his personality made up for his shortcomings in the physical realm. These were the variations he played: the PumpHouse and Cellblock, rather than the fashion show of the gay disco scene. Or the yuppie world of snazzy cars and fine fabrics; or the larvated, hidden desperation of the men in the redneck and blue-collar pubs of Fort Wayne or Oceanside, or Edina or River Rouge or Macon...

The tune ended, men began to disperse in the momentary hiatus, then a slow number began. Jerome looked at me questioningly, but I wasn't ready to snuggle up to his paunch and waltz. He put his arm around my waist as we left the dance floor, my troll-duty done. He wanted to hang beside me longer, but was gracious when I thanked him and turned to wander again. He was quickly into a conversation with another circle of PumpHouse regulars while I continued to study the crowd.

The 'Holden and Halsted' clones even moved and sounded like the Chicago boys; but they weren't. It was starting to get weird. I didn't think I could be that drunk already, only on my third beer in slightly more than 2 hours, but... damn! I decided to lay off awhile and cruise around the corral a bit more. Yup, on it went, *deja vu* all over again. There was a 'Mike,' and a 'Dan,' then a Tim and Luke and Tony, and yup there was even a Dean.

Holy shit...

That was no doppelganger.

It...

was...

Dean.

Dean Cordell, leaning against the corral rail, checking out the scenery, the men. I paused not eight feet from him, and did a fourth double-triple take. It was _him_. He was just as fine as ever, his snug jeans filled with that cock, the cock I'd remembered and fantasized so many times. The slightly thickened belly, the big arms, his hairy chest visible. He wore chaps and boots, a club vest with his badges and insignia, a navy blue bandanna in his left pocket... Oh yeah.

Dean hadn't yet seen me, or recognized me, whichever applied. I went back to the bar and ordered two bottles of Budweiser, making sure they had beer to go. With a little persuasion, I convinced the barman to put a 6 pack into a paper bag and keep it aside. I took my bottles back to the dance floor rail and came up from his blind side.

I leaned up next to him and the rustling of my leather got his attention. He turned, and I could see the wheels of his mind racing, digging... in a second, the memory was there, but not my name. I offered him a beer.

"The Maryland Hotel," he said. "Boy."

I smiled as he took his beer, and I raised mine to clink. "Daddy Dean, Sir..." and my voice did it.

"Matt."

We took a slow swig from the bottles, our eyes not breaking away. I continued.

"This scene gets old quick doesn't it?"

"Especially on holidays," he answered. "How about we get a few to go and head up to my room? Or up to your room?"

"Already ordered them Sir," I replied. "I thought you'd never ask." He grinned, grabbed my ass and pawed me, then pulled me in close, hot and hard. His kiss was salty, rough and masculine. He tasted of beer, smoke and testosterone. I held on tight, grinding against him hard. His bulge was already thickening. So was mine. My pride and the freedom of my epiphany filled me; if he'd asked me to strip and take his cock right then, right there, I would've complied instantly.

I was ready to go. We talked freely, but it took a full voice to be heard above the music. I noticed the big clock behind the bar now said 12:50; I wished him Merry fuckin' Christmas, and we kissed again.

"Um, how about a Merry Christmas <u>Fuckin'</u>?" I suggested.

"I thought you'd never ask," he answered, and we laughed heartily. "Where the hell you been, Boy? I expected to hear from you and never did."

"Well Sir, I can tell you all that's happened, but kinda tough in all this noise huh? Did you drive, or want to ride with me?" He had taken a cab to the Pump, so he didn't have to worry about driving he told me. "Cool, I'll drive. I'm at the Holiday Inn; wanna go there?"

He laughed aloud at that.

"Me too; room 241." The third door down from mine... yeah!

"Let's go Boy, I got something special for you." Together we went to the bar; Dean paid the bribe, $20 for the 6 pack. It wasn't that we needed the beer, but, we needed to do it this way. Carrying the paper sack discreetly, we headed to the door and out into the crisp, clear Christmas night.

Driving carefully back to the motel, I tried to fill him in on the events of the almost two years since we'd met in Chicago. I gave a quick run-down regarding Hennepin Terminal, the university, the men... only once I alluded to the Obsession he'd unleashed in me, but I waited, knowing I'd have to demonstrate more thoroughly, more convincingly once we were in the warm room and alone together.

I pulled into the cold quiet parking lot, just below our rooms. We embraced once more in the car, his hands groping me firmly, roughly. He pressed me back onto the carseat, kissing me deeply. I pawed his body, his belly.

"Sir, god Sir! I'm ready for you, I'm ready." He kissed me again.

"Sir, I'm thirsty..." I whispered. "I'm still thirsty for you Dean."

"Mmmmm,... yeah Boy, I'm sure you are. Let's get upstairs." We piled out of the car and quickly climbed the steps. An elevator scene would've been apropos, but in the cold and as, ahem, _full_ as we both were, it was no doubt for the best there wasn't one available. We were at my door.

"Do you need to get anything Sir?" I asked.

"Nothing that can't wait till tomorrow, Boy." Dean put his hand on mine and pushed the door open. We stepped inside and with a click of the lightswitch the darkened room was revealed. My street clothing and the selection of leather accessories lay atop the second bed, the jockstraps lined up for comparison. Dean glanced over it quickly, most of it didn't quite register.

He pushed the heavy motel door and it closed with a bang we barely noticed, already ripping off our jackets. Dean's hands were all over me, mine on him, groping and pawing, hugging and mashing together in lusty heat. My cock was rock hard, the front of his 501's proving him likewise. I groped his basket as he once more cupped my asshole in the palm of his hand. My jeans were tight, we had consumed 2 beers together and I'd had 3 others since I'd pissed. I assumed his load was like unto mine.

"Sir... oh man, SIR! Damn, I can't believe I found you here. But I'm so glad I did..." His smile was close and hot, my focus blurred being so close into his face. He sucked my tongue into his mouth as he pulled his denim shirt open, then off, not breaking our kiss while he did. Mine went next.

Tugging the flannel from under my belt, he pulled my bandannas out of the pocket. He looked at them with a smile.

"Left pocket huh? Lil' top-boy are you?" I grinned. "Well, not tonight... damn sure not top-boy tonight, _Boy_." His belt was unbuckled, the first 3 buttons of his jeans undone. Tufts of his thick fur were visible, he wore no unders. I stroked him slowly, then began to strip in haste.

"Sir... let's get naked, OK?" He nodded, the needs of our bodies over-riding our desire to peel our clothing and explore slowly. My boots were the tough part; by the time I got them off, Dean was naked, his thick cock standing out, ready for me, seeking the warm, wet confines of my mouth. I took him to the root as I wriggled out of the rest of my clothes.

I was on my knees as he began to fuck my face, drilling and jamming into my tonsils as I knew he would. Slurping him down as deeply as I could, I stroked myself in my spunky white strap. He bent over me slightly, rubbing his furry chest on my head, stroking my back. I pulled away from him and looked up into his blue eyes.

"Dean... Sir... I have something." His brow arched, he let me rise to show him. I slowly, deliberately reached across the bed to the arrangement of clothing, and slowly drew up that beautiful blue Bike jockstrap. I held it out to him, an offering, a sacred relic, my Holy Grail. "Sir..."

"Please, will you put it on for me again? Please Sir... I'm thirsty..."

The hot, lusty grin was unfeigned as he examined his jockstrap, stretching and feeling it. He stepped into it, then slid it up his body. The scent of dried, stale piss was heavenly. I all but swooned, knowing that the first donor, the _Author_ of it all was once more in it. His cock stretched the pouch to its fullest, his thick nuts shaping the lower line. He was glorious. In awe I admired him, worshipped him, and taking my hand he turned toward the bathroom.

I grabbed a new bottle of poppers from the sink vanity as we entered the tub-toilet room; in a moment the water was blasting hot, clouds of steam rising and softening the light. He pushed the showerhead to point down the wall as we stepped into the tub. Slowly, deliberately I slid down Dean's body, my tongue tracing the line between his mighty pecs, down his belly, to the edge of the jock, onto the fabric. I sucked and slurped, then leaned back to snort from my bottle. Dean put his hands on his hips, the head of his hard, massive tool just poking out the side of the pouch.

He watched as I hit, gently letting more and more of his dick stretch out, poke from under that smelly elastic. He reached and took the poppers from me, and with a slight pushing motion, thrust his cock toward me. I took him into my mouth again, savoring the mix of scent from his cock and balls, his sweaty bush and the blue Bike. He sniffed quickly, lightly, and let his eyes close as the rush overtook us both.

Sucking just the tip of his corona, I waited, the anticipation wilder, tenser, more pronounced than ever before. The *anticipation*, expectation was even more powerful and strange than the very first time I had awaited hot urine flowing from this very cock, this very penis, this man-feeder... I waited and suckled, my eyes closed and my hunger desperate. If he had pulled back and refused me, _denied_ me in that moment, I would've collapsed in tears and desperate pleas for the Nectar of my need: His _Piss_.

God, how I needed It! Right then I needed Him as I've never 'needed' anyone, anything before or since.

But he did not refuse me, he did not deny me. A trickle, a droplet and hot salty drooling formed on my tongue. I savored the teasing preamble, then I felt the tube of his cock thicken, widen and fill. His slit flared, opened and...

Piss.

Dean's piss, hot real piss. It flowed steadily, strong and fine.

He pissed; and my soul sang in satisfaction, in completion and gratitude.

Letting the thick salty silk fill my mouth, my hands gently held his balls. The flats of his meaty paws held my head softly, firmly, as his tube linked us, pouring his manly essence for me, into me. I slid his cock back and forth slowly as I regulated his flow, swishing piss around his organ, then had to swallow. A gulp, deep and full, then let him resume filling me.

"Ahhhhh, yeah Boy, that's it. Take it now, show me you're thirsty," he crooned softly. "Yeah Boy, there it is for you, drink it down, good Boy. *Drink me*..."

I gulped and swallowed more, more. I let his tube pour under full force, guzzling as I could, letting the rest shoot up behind my uvula. Piss ran from around my lips, down my chin and chest, onto my jockstrap. My cock throbbed, ached, strained in painful piss-lust as Dean fed me. I groaned, moaned lightly even as I drank him, drank his *piss*, his fluid, his masculine, hot *homo-sexual* output. I drank him in lust and in love, in a spiritual kind of union and communion as we shared this Obsession. Piss.

Once more I filled my mouth, then squeezed his dick, shutting off the flow. Letting his corona slip from my mouth, I looked up at Dean, holding his thick, salty and rich piss in my mouth. Quickly he helped me rise to share it, and in hot piss-kissing he too let a moan of piss-fulfillment escape from his strong chest. He hugged me tight, putting unbearable pressure onto my belly, my bladder.

"Come on Boy, come on... let it go..." he ordered, and his hand cupped my genitals as I relaxed and complied. "Yeah, yeah, yeah... that's it Boy, *piss* for me... *piss* for me..."

That 'for me' thrilled me, and I held onto him with love, feeling completed and fine as I gave him my juice too. The initial pressure was strong, I had to get past the burning <u>need</u> to piss, then I could slow the stream and enjoy it. Dean offered me the brown bottle, and I stopped my pissing while I took a snort. He reached around the curtain, looking about the bathroom. We'd brought nothing with us, no cup.

My heavy snorting finished, I gave the poppers back to the hot hunk with me and he hit deeply. Without a word, he was on his knees, pulling my strap aside and sucking on my hard cock. His left hand gripped my butt cheek, squeezing and kneading, as his right pressed onto my abdomen, encouraging me. I let it go... and Dean drank from me. I was feeding him, feeding <u>*us!*</u>

A gulp, another swallow, Dean took my piss, then let his mouth fill. Even quicker than he'd gone down on me, he rose and clamped his mouth on mine, shooting my piss between us. We shotgunned, swapped back and forth, licking and sharing it. Then I swallowed. He grinned at me, kissed me again.

"Don't get any stupid ideas because I took some piss from you, Boy," he growled, genuinely a bit embarrassed. We couldn't have him being self-conscious; I needed to clear this up quickly, get back into our lust and union.

"SIR! I know... it just means we've shared even more of each other, you're taking more from me, accepting me. I think it <u>*proves*</u> what I am and need, it certainly isn't going to rearrange our dichotomy." I doubted he knew the word, but I knew he'd like it.

"Good Boy, good... long as you <u>know</u> that. Now give me s'more." Once again he knelt to suckle and draw the masculine essence from me, from my cock. And again he rose to share a huge mouthful of my hot piss. Then I took his hard dick again, and he fed me. Back and forth, reversing roles we went, sharing in piss lust for a good 20 or 25 minutes. The control I'd learned (mostly from him in fact) was matched by his own. In all that time, urinating and stopping, flowing and slowing, pissing and feeding and sharing, we'd drained perhaps 2/3 of our loads. We both retained a substantial reservoir of piss for, ahem... later.

Without realizing it, I'd slid into that hyper-dimensional realm of no-time, of pure sex and pure homo- sexual lust. The moment of our piss could have been seconds, it might've been an aeon. My body thrummed in need, my asshole twitching. I rose once more, kissing Dean with a mouthful of his piss, then drew back. His hands still gripped my butt, but he'd not tried to invade me, penetrate or finger me. Yet.

"Sir?" I whispered, looking into his eyes.

"Sir... I need you. Please... _fuck_ me?" The obscenity, the sheer horny sexual desire of that whispered request whelmed us both. Asking this powerful, strong man to insert himself, insert his _penis_, his _cock_, into my rectum, to stretch and violate my anus, my _asshole_... Asking him, begging him to drive and drill himself into my body until he gave me his semen, until he couldn't hold back from enduring his orgasm, pumping the sacred masculine emission of his _balls_, his testicles, deep into my body. Begging for his sperm, his _Cum_... wanting and needing him deep within my rectum, my colon... to seed and breed me. Oh god...

He smiled slowly, eyes twinkling. As he'd directed me in previous encounters, so I told him, asked him, begged him openly, unashamedly, for what I wanted from him. I said it again.

"_Fuck_ me, Sir... please _fuck_ me..."

"Oh yes Boy, oh yes I'm going to fuck you. I damn sure _am_ going to fuck you Boy. Let's get out of here." He pulled the curtain aside and stepped onto the mat. We dried off quickly, the wetness on our bodies from steam and sweat, not pouring water. We remained sticky and scented as we returned to the bed.

Once more, incredible anticipation ran through me, my limbs literally quivering, shaking as we prepared for our copulation. I set fresh poppers and lube onto the nightstand, turning down the coverlet on the bed along the inside wall. My extra gear still lay atop the other, we ignored it for now. My ass was framed in the spunky elastic straps of my old jock, Dean's bulge cradled in the blue pouch of his... The bed ready, we climbed onto the crisp sheet and lay together, kissing and fondling.

His hand went below my nuts, a strong, thick finger finding the puckered ring of my hole. He probed gently, very tentatively, his dry skin scraping my anus. Dean didn't push into me at all, not wanting to relax my muscle. I knew exactly what he wanted to do; I wanted it too. He would not finger my asshole, he was going to open me up with his cock and only his cock. There would be no preamble to loosen me. I looked up at him as I lay on my back, my legs apart, vulnerable. His furred chest rose in hot breaths, his cock pointing up, out and up: it was a tool, the *weapon* that would conquer and subdue me.

Dean leaned over to kiss me, to stroke my body and licked down my chest to my hard, oozing cock. A gentle slurp and he took me into his mouth, sucking the drop of pearly precum from my piss slit. He gripped my balls, stroked me firmly then rose again, moving into position. He lifted my legs, wide, placing the soles of my feet onto his chest.

Framed in the 'v' of my own legs, Dean stood upright on his knees, his massive manhood threatening, promising, waiting... The fur on his chest was already matting in sweat, the room hot and close, our scent filling the air and each other's horny nostrils. He handed me the brown bottle, then smiled in a secret knowledge, his eyes narrowed.

"Boy, do you remember what I told you last time? When I left?" I paused, holding the poppers, and tried to recall. And then, I *remembered...*

"Yes... yes Sir, I do..." My sudden fear was not feigned.

I remembered our last fucking, and what he'd said at the door of room 1806.

"Good."

He grabbed the lube and slapped a gob onto my asshole, gave his cock a quick slicking of grease and placed his dickhead at my gate. He pushed my legs back hard, his hands gripping behind my knees tightly, firmly, painfully. He leaned forward, his corona just touching the ring of my asshole. I waited in fear and hope, in lust and need, I waited for what I knew Dean needed to do to satisfy himself.

And I needed him to do it to me, to complete my satisfaction as well.

"Take a snort Boy, take a BIG one."

I did, hitting four, fives times fully and deeply in each nostril. The sudden rush filled me.

I lay on my back, my legs being torn asunder, my asshole open and vulnerable to him, waiting for the inevitable.

LIKE THE TITAN

Dean glared at me, his eyes hot and wild, his intention clear. His powerful, incredibly hard nine-inch cock, fat and veiny, was poised at my asshole like a javelin, a lance, a sword... a spear. He intended to punish, to rape and rend, to impale me. He would crucify my body, and tear my soul apart as he did.

He was going to *hurt me*.

The power of that initial thrust was incredible, unbelievable, but so swift I did not know he'd even moved his hips. He thrust himself, shoved and entered at the very instant the poppers sent me into orbit.

My asshole ring parted as his corona slid into me, stretching the tight muscle of my sphincter. His cockhead passed through that wrinkly pucker and the nerves of my asshole sent a blast of warning, of pain, danger and fear coursing to my brain. The control centers of my body began to react, but already that hot, thick cock was sliding past the pucker and mashing against the wall of my rectum.

As the second inch of Dean's tool pushed into me, my asshole had gone from its automatic clench to an opening a full 3" in diameter within a tenth of a second. The vein along the upper side of his cock rubbed along my hole as his cockhead made contact with the back of my prostate. Another inch into me, the sensation of that collision washed across my consciousness.

Time slowed, the overwhelming power of this penetration ready to destroy me, to send me into unconsciousness. Dean's cock smashed behind my prostate, and continued into me, into me, opening me totally.

Four inches of male organ reached into my guts, and my reflexes finally began to stir. My legs tried to pull inward, to protect my body and my genitalia in that masculine reaction, but Dean's hot grasp held me taut, firmly. The fifth inch of dick tore into me, my asshole hot from the friction of his thrust. His cockhead oozed a tiny drop of precum as he violated my body, my being, my soul.

His cockhead was coursing fully seven inches within my ass, still on its forward, upward, inward mission to rend and ream. Dean's penis hit the end of my rectum yet the force was unabated as it stretched the upper curve of my tube and forced it aside. The puckered, slick wall of the gate to my colon slipped backward but could not resist. Dean's cockhead found the weak spot and entered.

As his stroke tore into my guts, the white-hot sensation of his destruction blocked out all other reality, and my diaphragm tightened to force a blast of air up and out my throat. My vocal cords snapped tight as the blast was forced up and out, the slow-motion sensation of my doom being matched by the low, almost soft and drawn out sound of my voice. It was not a moan, nor a gasp, but a full throated scream.

The last millimeters of that destroyer were forcing past my anus as his hot cockhead ripped into my colon, a full two inches past the inner hole. Tiny blood vessels burst, being ripped open and scraped raw along the walls of my rectum and inner workings. As the painful collision of Dean's pubic bone against me sent a new blast of neurological fervor, he was already reflexively reversing the direction of his rapine thrust, and pulling back.

His cock had slammed into me, his whole nine inches driven into me, into my guts in the most powerful, insane blast of sexual pain imaginable. I began to yell, to scream, but he held me down, wide and open. He thrust again, then forced my legs apart wider, and his second penetration was as rough, as powerful and destructive as the first. More.

I screamed, a full wail of pain and protest; but that was only an involuntary reaction. I *wanted* him to continue, to rape and destroy me in his lust, but I yelled, cried out in agony. I needed him to complete me. He thrust in, slamming his full length and weight into me and onto me yet again. I spread myself wider even as the reflex of my cries had not reached their apogee.

"AGGGGGGGGGGH! AHHHHHHHHHH! Sir, oh fuck SIR FUCK AGGGGGGGGGHHHHHHHH!" I screamed, and his eyes flashed in power and contempt, and with even more force his cock again ripped into my body, into my guts. Oh god it hurt, yet the reaction of my body, overwhelmed by pain and confusion, was to buck upward, to force against the intruder, to push harder onto him. I was torn asunder, violated and filled.

"SIR! Oh god SIR!" He ignored me, and with wild force and full thrusts began to fuck, to drive in and out, in and out of my asshole in power and violence. He fucked me, fucked me... he tore me open.

I tried to comply, to force myself into his desires, his fulfillment. My body, overwhelmed, tried to resist, but by sheer force of will I over-rode the pain and protest. I began to yell, to encourage him.

"It does NOT HURT... oh god Sir, it *DOES NOT HURT!*" He redoubled his powerful thrusting, reaming and parrying into me, pushing hard to one side then the other. His penetrations stretched my asshole open, stretched my rectum wide, forcing me to loosen and welcome his cock, welcome his essence and his being within me. He entered, invaded and filled me. It was as if he forced his whole Being into me, my body now housed us both as he fucked me.

"That's right Boy, tell yourself that. I know it *does*, goddam right!" he yelled. "Take it Boy, you should've CALLED ME BACK GODDAM

IT!" With another burst of unreal power, he once more slammed and fucked, raped me in violence and heat, in anger and power. In lust and his own completion...

"Fucker! SPREAD IT for me, yeah that's it. Yell and scream all you like goddam it, GIVE ME THAT ASS, BOY!" and the sounds of mashing flesh, of bone on bone and greasy cock slopping into my ripped-open asshole were all I could perceive. I forced myself open wider, spreading my legs.

"Yeah Dean! Yes Sir! Fuck me! FUCK ME SIR!" I bucked and tried to force myself to open farther, hoping his power and the depth of his fucking would grow, increase. "*FUCK ME!.*"

The gleam in his eye brightened, flashed in pleasure and hot union at my urging. Our coupling was solid, total as his cock rent and filled me, ripping into my bloodied guts again and again.

"*FUCK ME SIR!*" He growled, bucked and began to drive into me forcefully, holding 8" within my ass, and using just that last inch back and forth in hot, rapid, wild strokes, his corona completely within my inner hole, raping my colon. The pain was indescribable. *Pumpetty pumpetty pumpetty pump*, again and again as his cock swelled, his cum boiling in his balls, straining for release.

He yelled, slammed into me and fucked, reaming in frantic hot need. Pressing my legs back farther then ever, he reared up and in a flash smacked me hard across the face.

"Fucker! FUCKER! Fucking piss-boy, *fuck-boy*; take my COCK, *TAKE IT FUCKER*!"

Dean's eyes once more flashed and I knew it was upon us, my own cock hard and hot, pressed onto his belly with the force of his body pinning me to the bed. Pain metamorphosed into something else, beyond pain, into that realm of homosexual union, that higher plane of completion in power and lust. We passed that magical, spiritual line, and my body now floated, open and filled at once, the Being of 'Us' far surpassing the spirit of myself, of either of us alone. Dean felt too, whelmed as much as I was but sharing that Being from his side of reality, his Yin and my Yang joined, united.

He groaned, growled, and a primal urge and primal howl began to echo through the room. We yelled, we bucked and he fucked, fucked, _fucked_ me in wild ambition, his urge to destroy me coupled with the urge to complete himself, to complete the Duality, the _Us_. To be reborn with me in the union of our orgasm. He bucked again, then thrust in _hard_ and totally. He held me firmly, frozen, and howled as his balls split and he shot himself into my body.

"AAAGGGGH!" My howl echoed, reverberating from the hard block walls of the Holiday Inn. Dean's bellowing blended with mine, the cry of his hot orgasm ringing like that of a pikeman in battle, impaling me on his shaft.

"Goddam it Boy, goddam it! Fuck!" he yelled, and his dick shot wad after hot wad of thick semen deep within me. His neck resembled a channel of ropes, the cords standing taut and thick, etched as if carved in stone. His mouth was a grimace of agony, pleasure and agony. My own body resounded in harmony with his, my spunk exploding in a thick, hot arc up and across my chest as he poured and blasted his cum inside me.

"Take it Boy, I'm cumming I'm CUMMING! Oh fuck!"

"Sir oh fuck SIR! YEAH SIR I'M CUMMING TOO, oh fuck me Daddy, fuck me, fuck me _harder_ I'm CUMMING! Oh Daddy oh Daddy Daddy Daddy..."

"_DAA-AA-AA-AA-AA-AA-DDEE-EE-EEYYYY!_

The grunts and gasps of our insanity mingled, dwindled... as our dicks pulsed out the last gasps of our sperm, our lungs gasped for air as we sank into a heap of hot, sweating flesh, our bodies joined in full union. He collapsed atop me, his hands at last releasing their death-grips on the backsides of my knees.

My legs fell to the side, rubberized, useless. Dean's hefty body pinned me still to the bed, his cock remaining rock hard and buried in my asshole. Long moments ticked past as we lay, unable to speak, unable to fathom anything but the pure horny lust, the completion we had accomplished. The last droplets of our sperm leaked out, Dean's hidden within my receiving body, mine oozing lazily on my belly, the masses of my ejaculate gluing us together. Our gasping, raspy breathing slowed, at last becoming stable and normal again. Our eyes remained closed, the gleaming sparklers finally fading.

At long last I tried to move, rustling slowly against the sheet, against his hot body. Dean's eyes flittered open, and slowly, exhaustedly he pulled away from me, back and out. He rolled to his left, remaining facing me. I reached to stroke his chest, down to his cock. The wetness and slick feeling of his penis surprised me, I looked down.

My hand was coated bright red, his cock dripping my blood. His semen was mingled with it, thick gobby strands clinging to the sides of his shaft, my blood mashed into his bush. I took a quick breath, surprised. He was even more shocked than me when he saw it.

"Goddam it, Boy! *Goddam!* Are you OK? What the hell?" I touched my asshole, another glob of bright red blood came up on my fingers.

"Um, I don't know Dean. Um, Sir..." He was genuinely worried.

"What can I do Boy? That's not good..."

For some reason I knew it wasn't as bad as it looked, but the gore was actually somehow comforting, inspiring. He'd sworn to hurt me: his cock had actually stabbed me, wounded me, torn me open internally. I was not unhappy about it. Call it perversion, insanity, the Obsession... but I was _proud_ of myself. Proud of him, proud of myself...

Dean ran his hand onto me, trying to comfort me. I took his hand and reassured him.

"It's OK Sir, I'm OK. It'll be fine. Just relax..." I reached to the nightstand and took a cigarette. I offered one to Dean, but he declined. After just a couple drags, I moved to get up and he helped me turn to the side of the bed, gently assisting me. I rose and headed to the toilet.

Dean followed, but there wasn't much more to worry about. It had stopped and I fished a thick gob of his cum from my asshole, strings of my blood winding with and through it. Holding my two fingers up as I sat on the toilet, I laid it across my upper lip. Without a word, Dean leaned down slowly, tenderly kissing and sharing that hot, obscene outflow with me. I did it again. Like the vile Titan of centuries past, we ate our offspring, lest his ascendant power imperil our own. A moment later we returned to the bed.

I suggested we have more beer; hoping the idea of filling our bodies, our bladders would ease the tension. Indeed it did, and Dean grabbed two cold bottles from the sink where I'd left them in ice. We swigged. I gulped down half the bottle. He smiled, laughed and followed suit. In two minutes, we had a second bottle each, and drank slowly.

We had not completely drained when we'd arrived from the bar, even with all the pissing and sharing we'd done in the shower. Now we lay together, nuzzling and schmoozing, and the beer ran directly through us. I felt the pressure building in my lower belly and could only assume Dean was right with me. I ran my fingers gently on his furred abdomen.

"Dean, Sir? I'm thirsty... I'm still thirsty Dad..." He touched my face firmly, pulling me towards him, then planting a long deep kiss. I sucked his tongue, then pulled back.

"One thing though, Sir... I know we were wild, we <u>needed</u> that fucking just as violently as we shared it. But..." He looked at me intensely.

"You ever strike me again, for *any* reason, I'll fight back. I don't think I can 'win,' that's not the point. But I've had to throw it down more than once in the past, I know what I'm doing." He looked pensive.

"Real sorry Boy," he said. I nodded. "Just got wrapped up in it I guess..."

I wasn't being threatening or vindictive, but it was clear.

"Yeah, I know Sir. It's OK, I know what happened to you... to us. But I can't respect you and I won't tolerate you if you can't control that." Once more he looked away slowly, then kissed the tender spot gently.

"No more," he said. "Never again." I knew he meant it, and that was enough.

We finished our second bottle of beer, then began the third. My body was straining in piss-pressure, his must've been doing the same. We talked slowly, lightly as we recharged, both thirsty and ready to share our piss, our manly juices. He stroked me and pressed on my belly. The grunt I let out told him of my readiness. He rose from the bed first.

"Come here Boy, let your Dad have some of that hot piss." He knelt, between the beds.

I stood, my jock wet with piss and sweat, the years of service it had seen exuding hot manly scent. My cock was half-hard, thick and long but pliable. Dean took me gently, sucking slowly to the root and back. Taking the poppers once again, I huffed slowly, a nice full hit, and gave them to him. He took a hit, then positioned my corona just inside his lips. I relaxed and began to flow.

Piss, my piss shot in a nice steady stream into his thirsty mouth. He drank, savoring my sweet beer piss. He gulped, swallowed again and again, his bladder filling from the influx of my fluid with his beer and his own kidney function.

He drank several good mouthfuls; then I stanched the flow. He looked up, my dick still in his mouth, the pensive look of a man sucking a dry cock was strange, interesting. I motioned him to rise.

"Let's lay together Sir, I want to take as I receive." He thought that was a *great* idea and we moved to the open bed, the scene of our violent sodomy, a red smear marking the place of my birthing. Slowly, as in tandem, we moved into a 69 and took each other's cocks into our mouths. I closed my eyes, and together, with a silent, gentle rush our bodies joined.

We pissed together, drinking and pissing, feeding and filling each other at the same time. Completion. We were joined: and each had found that *same*, that *likeness*, his *homo*-. We were homos, his cum within my ass, my cum coating us both as we shared our piss. It was sublime, indescribable, unique.

What had begun in fear and trepidation, the perversion of piss-lust overwhelming me in that Chicago shower-stall had come full circle. I'd gone to the depths of depravity and self-loathing, yet emerged stronger, triumphant for it. The very one who had first unleashed, released and revealed the Obsession again joined me, sharing and rejoicing in our lust, our secret hunger and fulfillment. He understood what we shared. In that night, we loved one another as never before, and never since. A love of 'self,' and a knowing, open love for each other that can never be duplicated. Nor would either of us want it to. We took what we had, and gave it to each other.

Pissing and drinking, drinking as we pissed, our link was complete. Our bladders emptied into one another, then at long last we kissed, our arms reaching between our legs, holding hairy bodies and dripping manly organs together. Finally I rose, cleared the other bed and prepared to end the night. There wasn't even a suggestion that we rinse or remove the markings of our union, and we got into bed sticky and scented. We lay together, holding each other lightly as we drifted into a long, deep and peaceful Christmas sleep.

COMPLETION

I awoke that Christmas morning before Dean, still sticky and smeared with our fluids. It was beautiful, and I once more touched my fingers to my asshole, checking for further bleeding. I was OK. I rose quietly, and slipped into some jeans and shoes to go get us some coffee from the motel lobby. He was still snoring softly when I returned.

Placing the cups on the small table, I quietly slid back into bed with the hot man. Nuzzling against him gently, he woke, looking at me with a groggy smile.

"Merry Fuckin' Christmas Sir," I greeted him. He wrapped an arm around me and shoved me under the cover. His cock was funky, hot and sweaty. It lay thick and sticky on his leg, already half hard. He was full and pushed me toward his needy dick.

"Drink me Boy, drink your morning treat..." he said. I took him into my mouth, the sheet and blanket tenting me as I suckled. In a moment, his piss was flowing up and into me, as I'd also drank him in Chicago. I gulped the thick, hot liquid; yellow and rich, golden and salty. I drank, gulping slowly, savoring his manhood as he fed me.

"Yeah Boy, that's it, drink me down." He pumped another hot burst up into my willing mouth, and I swallowed, then slurped him off. Finally I emerged from my tent and faced him.

"Mmmmmm, yeah! Thank you Sir!" He grinned. "You want some too?"

His smile fell slightly, he was nonplussed.

"Um, I don't think I want morning piss there Boy, that's not... um..." I stopped him.

"It's OK Sir; I understand. I like your piss anytime, even first thing in the morning. Besides, we were drinking beer; it's not like waking up after a meal of roast beef, potatoes and asparagus..." He laughed aloud.

"Yeah, I guess it is just beer piss, isn't it?"

"Well, it's rather more than watery beer piss, Sir, but... it was... *wonderful*." I kissed him without tongue, both of us needing our morning toilette prior to that.

He lifted himself up on one elbow.

"Then get those fuckin' jeans off and let me have some, Boy. I'm ready."

Quickly I got up and naked, then laid on the other bed. I lifted my cock, offering the sweet delicious nectar I held. Dean stretched alongside me, recumbent as I'd done with him. He stroked up and down my dick, then tentatively took the head into his lips. He closed his eyes, in that sublime anticipation we know so well. In beautiful expectation he waited, then I opened to him. My cock flexed, my bladder tightened as my urethra opened and began to flow.

Piss, he sucked my piss; hot thick, morning piss.

With a low moan, his eyes fluttered as his first mouthful sent waves of hot scent and salty goodness into his sinuses, the taste filling his mouth. He gulped, then shoved himself onto me fully, then stroked back, letting my pissing cock pour my urine up for him, filling his mouth.

He slurped and gulped, drinking and guzzling fast and fully. I stopped the stream, holding back. He looked at me, waiting, then dropped my cockhead from his lips.

"Oh man... Boy, that's not all you've got is it?"

"No Sir, it's not. There's plenty more. I wanted to taste you, taste with you..." He smiled, then returned to my dick. I opened again, letting a slow stream fill him, then stopped again. He lifted up, moved into a full kiss and spewed my piss into my mouth. Silken, heavenly, thick and salty... I swished it around then returned it to him. Once again he shotgunned back to me, and I let it slowly run from the corners of my mouth, wetting my body. He gasped in horny joy, then once more sucked. I pissed, letting it shoot hot and fast, not controlling it at all.

Overwhelmed in it, piss ran over us both, wetting the bed, wetting his body hair. He gulped as he could, wallowing in it all. Piss. Piss, he loved it as I did.

The full stream poured for him and he fed. As always, it tapered off, then I gave that fine final spurt, He was sated. He rose up and lay atop me, grinding his body against me as we kissed, piss wetting us both. Our piss-union completed, at last we rolled apart and I offered the coffee, cooled but still fine to drink. We relaxed, talked.

There was a lot to catch up on, and Dean was interested in all of it. The transfer terminal, the summer... the Delta Tau fraternity party. He was astounded, amazed, all but uncomprehending. The sheer magnitude, the power and majesty, the total piss-glory of it. He was filled with admiration.

"My god Boy! *Thirty-three* of them? *All night?*" I smiled, grinned and nodded. I tried to explain the horrible emotional wranglings of my Purgatory; then the Resurrection, the Epiphany I'd experienced in the trough. He followed, comprehending fully.

"So, that's kind of how and why I wanted, why I *needed* that beautiful fucking we had last night Dean. You'd said, next time you'd *hurt me*, and you did. You tried. But..." I paused, his knowledge dawning bright and glorious. "I survived it. _We_ survived that too." Once more, naked with this man, I was proud, defiant and proud, my Obsession and its fulfillment my crown. I owned it, owned up to it, embraced it and made it sacred.

"Man..." he whispered. "God, I'd love to try that. I don't know if I could endure like that though..." He trailed off. His own longing was clear, but his trepidation was too. I knew his thoughts ran as mine had, when I'd watched Carl in that trough in Chicago. *Someday... maybe someday...*

The hour progressed and the room phone rang, a desk clerk telling me we were past check-out. Dean wasn't having it. "It's Christmas Day!" he said. "Where the hell are you going to go, do what? We're staying right here!" He offered to get his bags, he'd not even unpacked, and move to my room. I had a better idea.

"I'll throw my shit together and we'll take *your* room; let the 'Señorita' clean this one!" We laughed; Dean called the desk clerk, and that's exactly what we did. We dressed quickly, jockstraps and jeans, shoes and jackets. He paid for another night in the motel-room, and I moved my gear down the balcony walkway to number 241.

Once in his room, we decided food was in order. A few phone calls yielded a pizzeria that was actually open and delivering on Christmas Day. We ordered, requesting other supplies as well. The delivery man himself came on the line, and with assurance of sufficient 'recompense' agreed to stop at the convenience store for us.

He brought us a large pie, soda, cigarettes... both Dean and I'd somehow forgotten basic toiletries, so the delivery guy also brought 2 toothbrushes with the mini tubes of paste. I told him the story of the

Chicago Nightmare; he howled with laughter.

But through the talk, the time and food, the intimacy, we were still charged with nothing but pure hot homo-sexual wants and needs. The prospect of *fucking*, of cocks and cum, of sweat and testosterone and piss was what had united us at the beginning; it still did.

"So you think this whole thing, this obsession, is seeking something, someone just like yourself? Seeking yourself? Is that how it works?"

"Well yeah kind of, but not your SELF, rather, one *like* you, one who appreciates and shares your obsessions, relates to them, but is counterpart in them. Like you and me... your hot fat cock needs a wild, horny hole. And I have that; we click. But even though you're top and I'm bottoming, we're not really different. The *action*: we're seeking the same thing really."

"Yeah OK... I think I get most of what you're saying. Way too fuckin' philosophical for me though. I just like to fuck, and I like when you drink my piss..." I had to chuckle at that. Nobody could accuse Dean Cordell of being glib.

He paused a moment. "Speaking of piss..." His beautiful eyes twinkled.

We were stripped to our jockstraps in a second, and again I knelt to take his piss.

The whole day and night way took turns pissing, drinking, kissing. It was past dark when we decided to fuck again, the wild, insane needs of the night before abated. Dean took me slowly, gently, the first time the two of us had actually taken time and enjoyed the act of opening, of penetration and our coupling. His cock slid into me deeply, fully as always, but instead of the white hot lightening, the sensation was otherworldly, intense and fine. I spread for him and he buried again into my inner hole, fucking as we looked into each other's eyes.

His cock slid back and forth, in and out in slick greasy man-fucking, we shared poppers but not like we so often had before. They were an augment, a treat. The way we'd fucked in the past I'm sure I couldn't've endured him power-pounding me with that massive cock without them. He turned me, pulling back but not removing himself from my hole, then I lay on my belly, offering my ass to him.

He drilled into me deeply, and we shared another powerful, total orgasm. I lay prone with Dean atop me, my buns mashed up against his belly, his penis buried deep within me. I felt as he opened his valve, and hot piss pumped into my recesses, flooding my guts and filling me.

"Oh yeah man, yeah... give it to me..." I moaned softly, taking everything he could give. He filled me, the palms of his hands on the backs of mine, our fingers interlaced. We moaned softly and sensuously came together. After giving me his cum, sharing in mine, he went to the bathroom with me. Unashamedly I sat on the toilet, my legs spread wide, and we watched in hot, perverted lust as his load of piss and cum poured from me. I moaned and yelled in obscene labor, giving birth. I wanted him to suck it from me, to spew it back and shotgun, to drink his piss from my own asshole... but he didn't move to felch me and I said nothing.

Someday...

Our philosophical discussion continued late into the night, the nature of the Obsession was fascinating to him. Far from shallow, he actually related completely well to what I was trying to describe. Dean enjoyed it thoroughly, proud and heady, that I considered him the instigator, the Author of my Obsession in piss. He shared it with me, in all regards.

"You know, I've been trying to wrap my head around some of these ideas for some time. And like flipping the switch here, I think... you know, I'm going to let myself explore. I want to experience some of that joy, that freedom you're talking about."

I wondered at this. As with many a hot 'top,' he simply needed the right combination of circumstances, of need and opportunity, to turn and experience the other side. He'd done so in drinking and sharing my piss; now he was talking about opening up, finding someone truly like unto himself, taking another hot, violent man's cock raping and reaming him senseless. He wanted it, he needed to have it. He could share my piss, tell me his secret needs... but I was not yet the man to fuck him. That would have to wait.

Pissing and fucking, sucking and tasting, we spent hours naked, penetrating and sharing. The variation played itself out between us in that motel-room as Christmas Day had dawned cold and bright, and slid into December 26th in darkness and the warmth of our sexual union. It was past midnight when we slipped into a satisfied, deep sleep. Dean snored beside me; I floated in exhausted joy, my belly filled with his piss.

We awoke late, took our time packing up and this time, as equals, we made our departure. I drank his load of piss one last time and he took mine. We swapped our contact information, kissing deeply and talking softly. Changing clothes for the road, I noticed we were both marked with the nubby imprints of our jocks; once more, branded. Jockstrap-branded as I should be. We checked out of the Holiday Inn and waved as we pulled from the parking lot. Getting onto the Interstate, we drove along for a good piece on the same highway, then our roads parted.

The metaphor was apt. We'd come from disparate origins, converged, then traveled together for part of our journey. Though the road we took joined, ran the same course for a time, we were not on the same path, the same 'highway.' The high points, the landmarks along this path had meant different things to each of us; and now they pointed us in different directions. We approached a major junction.

I took the right hand fork, Dean the left. I headed back to Fort Wayne, and he to Illinois.

My asshole throbbed as I drove on, contemplating those holiday nights. Our accomplishment was sublime, and I basked in post-coital pride. I burped: a beautiful, heady piss-burp. *Dean's piss!* I chuckled and savored the taste of his manly flow as I drove on, knowing he was savoring mine as well.

The circle was completed.

INTO THE FIRE

The next week back in the Fort was uneventful. I saw Jack, my neighbor, from my window. He still ignored me, unable to come to terms with the obsessions that haunted him. I made eye contact with him, but he never so much as waved. Should he ever manage to accomplish a resolution in his own mind, he'd know where to find me.

New Year's Eve was upon us, and with several acquaintances from the University, I made plans to ring in 1981 there in Fort Wayne. It would be leather and hardware for me, gay formal for Chris, who knew what kind of punk regalia for Tommy? We planned to meet at Up the Street around 9:00. My apartment was reasonably close, but I'd taken a room at a nondescript downtown hotel anyway. No drunk-driving arrest was needed, and having a discreet (*neutral!*) room might mean the difference between finding a companion for the night and not.

The crowd was festive as we arrived, already quite full attendance. I glanced about the lounge, then headed into the back room, to the dance floor. A wooden corral-rail ran around three sides of it, the bricked room rising 2 stories. Disco reflections and colored lights, there was something satisfying and generic about the whole picture. The festive New Year's Eve hats and leis, noisemakers and trinkets were the same supplied in many pubs that night... it could've been any of them, all of them.

Men danced and drank, talked and circulated. Lovers kissed and groped, friends schmoozed, new acquaintances got intimate. Tommy and Chris quickly were off with newfound friends; ready to become intimate and primal themselves.

I looked at closely at the patrons.

There was a Tim and a Joe. A Mark and Dave and Marky J; a Tommy and Tony and even a Dean. Beyond them another Halsted and Holden pawed at each other, 'Holden' then sank to his knees in front of the other, mashing his face onto the full bulge under hot denim. Someone giggled just behind my right shoulder.

"Oh I love it; *prick worship!*" he chuckled. I laughed too.

"Yeah, but the scene gets kind of tired doesn't it?"

He agreed. "Tell me about it, I fuckin' work here!" His black T-shirt advertised the bath-house in Indy, the BodyWorks.

"Is that a name or a guarantee?" I asked him.

"Well, it's a name, but yes, the body *does* work." We clicked, and soon I was groping him through his Levi's. He responded quickly, ready for a private New Year's Eve celebration at the Double L Motel. To show me, he knelt and mashed his face onto my jeans, reaching up through my chaps and fondling my belly. Thus he was on his knees and worshipping my cock as the countdown ended, and 1981 began with a toast. I pulled him to his feet for a long, deep kiss.

"Happy New Year! Let's get a couple of beers to go," I said, "Then head back to my room and get my cock up your ass." He giggled again. Hot, well-defined body, tight full pouch in his jeans, his nice round buns were ready for a full-court press.

"I thought you'd never ask," he said. "But I've got to finish up here, it'll be another hour at least." I scowled at his answer.

"Someone else is playing the records now; you know damn well he'll be happy to finish up the DJ thing. Get your crap and let's go. _Do it!_" He giggled again.

"Well, since you put it that way, Sir... OK." He went up to the DJ booth and hustled his gear into a box. Within 3 minutes, he was back down with me and we headed out into the snowy night. He rode in my car; the motel only 5 blocks away. We passed a cop on the first block, administering a field sobriety test; and another situation on the second. I drove slowly, carefully, and we arrived. I ushered him up to my room, the windows steamy from the heat within.

The heat was definitely 'on' in there, we were stripped in seconds. I admired him; a bit shorter than me, he was nicely formed even if a bit on the fleshy side. His pecs were thick and smooth, and his arms hefty and defined. His cock curved upward, hot and ready. Wrapping my arms about him, we kissed and pressed our flesh together. He pawed my jockstrap, the latest one I'd taken from Dean. I moved him to the bed and we linked in a tight, deep-throating 69. My body was telling me more though, and in only a few minutes I pulled him up from the bed and led him to the bathroom.

The shower spurted hot, steam quickly filling the enclosed place. He liked it, and we stepped into the tub and closed the curtain. My cock throbbed hot and slick, his slobber greasing me. I handed him the poppers and pressed suggestively on his shoulder. He sank to his knees, then hit the amyl. Taking my dick into his mouth as he swooned, he sucked, gulping me to the root. His own dick jiggled and pulsed, jumping up and down, hard and slick too.

He sucked me, and I hit the poppers. I pulled back from him, holding my cock at the base. He looked up at me, wondering, as I took slow aim at his chest and let my stream open up. He gasped.

Piss. There it was.

"Ohmigod! Oh! God!" He watched in rapt horror and fascination as the stream played onto his chest, up and down him, wetting his manhood, his body. "Wow, that's wild! We're really into the fire tonight, huh?" I stopped pissing, and spoke firmly.

"Lean back, and *open... your... mouth!*"

His eyes widened in fright bordering on pure terror, but... he leaned back. I opened my valve and pissed, my aim dead-on. Into his mouth. He held it, not moving.

"Now then, swallow it. *Swallow it.*" He closed his mouth and gulped.

"Good boy, good. Here, here's the amyl. Take another hit. What's your name, Boy?'

Holding the wet bottle in shaking hands, it was all he could do, my piss dripping from his smooth chin, to answer.

"Bruce... Bruce..."

"Bruce; that's nice, Boy." He nodded. "Now then Boy, here... hit that bottle and *suck me.*" He opened the cap and took a hit, another, a mighty hit... and I took it from him as I slipped my cockhead between his quivering lips.

"Now then Boy, get ready. Drink it, here... *drink me.*"

His eyes closed as I opened up and pissed for him, pissed to him, in him. He drank, swooning and gulping. He took it, the rapture of his countenance sending me as he drank, drank and his hence-unknown need, his dark, secret thirst was slaked. He gulped, and I stopped the flow.

"Ohmigod, oh... oh my fuckin GOD! Oh man, that's... it's... *Oh fuck that's hot!* Can I have more? Please? More?"

I smiled and nodded. "Sure you can Bruce."

"What's your name?" he asked. Carefully he reached up and took my cock, cradling the shaft and pointing the slit at his own tongue.

"Um, Bruce... *Boy*... you call me *Sir*."

"*Yes, Sir,*" he whispered. "*Yes, Sir.*"

He waited expectantly, unmoving, hoping and waiting... needing. His eyes were *pleading* for me to quench his now-desperate thirst. I placed my corona just into his lips, then paused.

"OK good, good Boy. Now here you go. Nice and slow. Drink me Boy, drink it down. That's right, you take it now, show me how much you like it. That's it, good Boy... *Ahhhhh...*" His grunting and moaning even with his mouth filled with my cock, gulping and savoring in that hot shower told me far more. His eyes slowly fell closed as he nursed, suckled in pure homo-sexual joy and completion.

I held his face gently as I fed him, my piss filling and fulfilling him, filling the emptiness he'd not even known was there. The night would go on, there was so much to learn.

Piss.

Out of the frying pan and into the fire, the Obsession was born in another.

EPILOGUE

Bruce and I saw each other regularly over the next 3 years. He learned the joys of piss, learned to share his obsession and focus it, use the knowledge for his own advantage. He included me in many important events in his life, and helped me to become a member of the 'Community' while I remained in graduate school.

We both developed other relationships, long term commitments that our mutual infatuations weren't necessarily a main aspect to. We shared the Obsessions with each other: our jockstraps and piss were always the centerpiece of our hot intercourse. He became utterly fascinated with taking my piss up his ass; and he carried a full load of it within his colon at the Commencement when I received my Doctorate. My academic finery concealed a coating of piss and cum on my body, my yellow jockstrap crusty and clinging beneath my regalia.

Dean kept his word to stay in touch, and as with Bruce, I was along for many significant, seminal events in his life and development. Following our Christmas meeting, he invited me to stay with him in Chicago for the long weekend of IML, which had become 8 days by the time it was ended. He had ideas about his own piss-trough scene, but was too much the macho-man to allow the Chicago queens to know he'd flipped, becoming a piss-pig of the first echelon.

Making a few fast inquiries, by the time I'd been with him another 36 hours we were on our way to New York, for a long night at the legendary MineShaft. A friend of a friend had an 'in,' and a scene on the order of my Piss Purgatory was arranged. He was fearful, filled with foreboding and trepidation, doubting his own sanity. But as had happened with me, once the wheels had been set in motion, it was inexorable: he had to go through with it.

The deluge of piss obsession, of heavy, testosterone-charged leathersex and the new and intense variations he played on his obsessions following his 'party' were enough to fill several books, and perhaps someday they will be written. His party involved him in a semi-public club with more than 80 men present, although those actually participating in his piss-scene were probably about 30, much as mine had been.

But from that, his fascination and imagination went into higher gear. He often consulted with me and tried new and exciting variations with me first. He'd accepted me as an equal when we'd left Indianapolis; now he submitted to me as one who understood his needs, understood his obsessions even better perhaps than he did himself. He explored sounds and catheters, group scenes and heavy bondage, fisting and double penetrations... piss and perversions on a magnificent, new scale.

The newfound openness and easy sex of the early 1980's though came to a crashing end with the onset of AIDS and the Reagan years. I've never been convinced those are connected phenomena, but I'm not convinced they aren't. In any case, the nameless sexual riotry and endless experimentation stopped. But not before some other fascinating and wild expressions of our Obsessions were brought to fruition in glorious, living Technicolor.

Such as the night Dean lay strapped in a sling, his body supported by two hot leather daddys while I and yet another worked him over. With the creative use of a catheter and some toys, I rigged him to piss into his own ass, filling himself with a quart or so of hot, rich piss.

Later, using a variation of that same device, he bellowed in horny agony as he lay, helpless, bound and violated, and the full load of my piss flowed unabated directly into his body, into his bladder.

"HURT ME!" he screamed, and embraced his needs and his obsessions in glory. In pain and submission he found a new and fuller expression of the transference of power and dominance he'd always sought in imposing his will, his body and his fluids, onto other men. Far from exchanging his power for subjugation though, it completed him, and set him free.

But those Chronicles are for another time, another journey. That is the story of Dean's freedom. While he is indeed the one who first set the ball in motion for me, his story is not mine. Seeing him screaming and writhing as he endured violation and submission in piss and overwhelming perversions, I realized that my story was, for the most part, completed.

Of course my obsessions, my Chronicles continue, and I'd have it no other way. But they are variations, exploration of insight and Truth already fulfilled. For that, and for opening the door leading to that Truth, I will always thank and remember Dean.

AUTHOR'S NOTE

I am quite sure it will be obvious to most readers that the events, characters and locations depicted in _The Yellow Jock Chronicles_ are for the most part genuine. And as usual, names have been changed, dates and locations modified. Some are composites, others purely fictional creations suggested by one or more real person, place or event. That's the beauty of retelling what is, in greatest part, a true story, but with the license to adapt and modify according to literary need.

Resemblance to real persons, living or dead, is a matter of degree. Those persons most responsible for and most involved in the actual events described herein may or may not recognize themselves and others. But to them and to all, I wish to say that no offense is intended in descriptions of human weakness, mistakes or deeds which may have caused anyone harm or distress. The events are far in the past; those who would fault me for the fictionalized version of what might or might not have happened in real time need to find something else to bitch about.

I ask readers to take the book for what it is: the reflections of one person put into a kind of context that may or may not make sense to others. In the meanwhile, I hope what I have set out is an entertaining and enjoyable story, if not one which a particular reader can relate to or derive any new "enlightenment" or such therefrom.

Those who read this account with an open mind and interest in their own predilections will, I think, relate to the struggles and the dawning self-awareness I have tried to describe. Perhaps my *Chronicles* will give cause for reflection, perhaps it's just a good wild pornographic story... but I ask readers to realize that while what I have written may have been "real," it is presented through an admittedly very selective filtering process.

Some events are presented quite accurately, others as they "should have" happened, still others as I "wish" they had happened; and lastly, some events and characters are nothing but the fruit of a beautifully perverse and creative imagination, "fiction" in the purest sense.

M. M. Schiffmann

Richmond, Virginia

ABOUT THE AUTHOR

Matthew Schiffmann has been publishing books and articles since the mid-1970's under several names. An accomplished professional musician, Dr. Schiff has performed across the US and Canada as both pianist and conductor. His published writings range from social and political science materials to theological analyses, poetry and fiction. His homo-erotic fiction resumes after a long hiatus with the release of _The Yellow Jock Chronicles_.

From very small-town roots through advanced studies in major Universities and academies, Schiff has an extremely wide background. The range of his interests can be surprising: he has earned citations in automobile and motorcycle restorations, professional tailoring, business projects involving major automobile manufacturers and international banking, and is accomplished in several other fields. His students have generally regarded him as one of the most formative figures in their education. He has taught subjects ranging from mathematics and natural sciences, music, to classical languages and theology, spanning classrooms from kindergarten through doctoral–level students.

Dr. Schiffmann's social involvement includes working for removing barriers based upon sexual orientation, and has served in top-level consultation for State and local government agencies. He is currently working with the Equality Project, and is producing the framework and legal basis for major civil-rights litigation.

Matthew Schiffmann is also the author of:

The Yellow Jock Chronicles - Volume One: Jockstrap Epiphany A Journey into Self-Awareness, Discovery and Acceptance: An Obsession with Jockstraps and Piss-Lust

(978-1-934625-28-6, The Nazca Plains Corp., 2007)

Available from Amazon.com, Goodboner.com, or your local bookstore.

www.ingramcontent.com/pod-product-compliance
Lightning Source LLC
Chambersburg PA
CBHW071207260626
47162CB00004B/1205